eva sallis

fire fire

First published in 2004

Allen & Unwin
83 Alexander Street
Crows Nest NSW 2065
Australia
Phone: (61 2) 8425 0100
Fax: (61 2) 9906 2218
Email: info@allenandunwin.com
Web: www.allenandunwin.com

National Library of Australia
Cataloguing-in-Publication entry:

Sallis, E.K. (Eva K.).
Fire fire.

ISBN 1 74114 352 7.

I. Title.

A823.3

Set in 11.5/16 pt Granjon by Asset Typesetting Pty Ltd
Printed in Australia by McPherson's Printing Group

10 9 8 7 6 5 4 3 2 1

For L'hibou and Bodie

Still at large

acknowledgments

Thanks to Annette Barlow, Anne Bartlett, Kirsty Brooks, Rose Creswell, Sophie Cunningham, Jenni Devereaux, Mariana Hardwick, Sue Hosking, Annette Hughes, Maria Joseph, Stephanie Luke, Bryan Lynch, Gay Lynch, Heather Millar, Anna King Murdoch, April Murdoch, Roger Sallis, Tom Shapcott, Morgan Smith, Julia Stiles, Mandy Treagus, Colette Vella, Phil Waldron and Teresita White. Thanks also to Richard, Briar, Erika, Barbara, Alfred, Konrad, Richie, Robbie, L'hibou and Michael.

A version of 'Topend' was published in *Elle* in 1999 as 'Summer Goes North'.

A work-in-progress version of 'Dirige Dominus Deus Meus' was published in *Southerly* in 2003.

The Tomten is a book by Astrid Lindgren. The nightingale song is a traditional German folk song.

contents

prélude

The doorframes buckled and split. Struts melted and curled. Paint peeled back, revealing little dramas along the architraves. The bared white wood turned gold, crazed and black in seconds, then spat jets of blue and orange. The kitchen, the first room roofless, roared like a wind tunnel, cooking the stacked dirty saucepans until they folded in on themselves and formed white-hot aluminium patties. The floor rose to meet the flames, as if something invisible were shouldering its way out from underneath the house, issuing from the flowering floor, making a grand appearance. Then the kitchen windows exploded, scattering shards of hot black glass over the garden, scorching the roses and Christmas lilies. The head-height cupboards opened their mouths, red and roaring, and vomited three decades of photos, albums, certificates, scrapbooks, sketches, locks of hair and other detritus into the updraught of the flames. The table suddenly cracked in the middle and heaved dark thighs into the flames. The roof of the house lifted, flapped dark wings once before it crashed onto the wilting garden in a pile of shrieking galvanised iron.

In the light-scalded auditorium, the instruments flared in their corners. The cello's golden varnish was a silk scarf whipped away and then the cello belched and burst. Violins curled like babies on the roaring sofa.

Small creatures, frozen into doorframes and cornices, came to life and began to sing. They hissed and farted, sizzled and sighed, whispering joyously around the walls as the fire reared fifty metres into the air. Listen listen listen, the voices muttered, licking their lips before they too, one by one, bucked, bent their backs and flew screaming skywards.

Scorched photos winged with flame were puffed into the sky, then floated away. Faces smiled up at the blue, as the horses, goats, dolls and the siblings they hugged or held were eaten away from their arms. Charred and separated fragments of the Houdini family fell softly, like black snow, on the surrounding bush.

aubade

'We are internationals, transnationals,' Acantia said, twisting around, catching each child's eye from the front seat of the kombi. 'But we are retreating from the world and we must find the right place for us to live out our days in *full* creativity. All the spiritual masters and the great artists retreat from the world.'

Her eyes were a little square, like those of a cornered cat, and Pa looked resolute. The kombi passed mountain fortresses, their damp and rotting timbers barely visible among the tall trees, passed cavern houses hidden behind cliff faces. The kombi passed by endless expanses of stubble and a sequence of ruined stone, brick, slate, weatherboard and battered tin, and other piles of broken rooms. The kombi, lined with the faces of the five children and baby, passed by a low green cottage and sheds in the dunes on the edge of a great grey lake.

It had to be something extraordinary.

Acantia made an adventure of it but the children sensed something underneath.

They had left the great world in a great hurry.

Pa was very big: Acantia looked like a dwarf next to him on the front seat. Pa drove the kombi but they all knew that Acantia chose the direction. Pa found their house, finally, but Acantia chose it. When they first rattled along the bush track to Whispers they found themselves facing something very unusual indeed. The house was a strange conglomeration, partly an old hall, the former residence of a bankrupt named Angus Bad, secreted on a large bushland property in the hills near the city of Toggenberg. The grey and brown trunks of the stringybarks surrounded it like an army weathering a long siege. They were lean and spare and hardened. The birds fell silent as the Houdinis, twigs and dried gum leaves crackling under the tyres, wound their way along the disused bush track. Pa stopped the kombi and the children listened. The bush gave off faint snapping and intermittent crackling sounds, like sentinels easing their knee joints and cracking their jawbones. It was late spring and the early heat shimmered through the limp grey and red leaves, which seemed to wriggle and writhe out of the corner of the eye.

The birds started up again, cautiously, and the sentient sounds of the bush were swallowed.

Ursula pressed her nose to the filthy window and felt her snot sucker her nostrils to the warm glass. She stared out, wondering and wondering. It was a hideaway, for sure. You could sense that people were things of the past, that no foot had trod, and that not many, other than the Houdinis, would want to. On balance, she liked it. She had a sudden image of herself, unkempt and twiggy, with a long beard and goatskin clothes, chasing lizards. The last survivor. Yes, she liked it. What she wasn't so sure about was why they were here. The great world had seemed benign: just music and concerts and people eating undersized sausages with thumb and forefinger. There were also the bodgies, widgies, druggies, bra-burners, no-hopers, home-breakers, double agents, fifth columnists, reds and lefties, but they were easily dismissed, always had been. Acantia had no fear of them, and neither had Ursula.

How could Acantia know that the great world hadn't come with them, like a disease in her and Pa? In the kids? What if Acantia had overlooked their permeability? Maybe it was here already waiting in the gaunt trees. It was the retreat that troubled Ursula, not the world. Was retreat possible? Did the world just stay put once it had become mysteriously threatening? Was there a border between worlds?

Acantia should know.

Pa hummed Mozart sonata melodies as he stared up at the caved-in ceiling of the auditorium. He grinned at the children conspiratorially as he opened and shut the broken front door, stomped the rotted pathways, shook the trees, jumped on the floorboards. On the verandah he waved his arms at the sky, the bushland, the great trees, the absence of prying human eyes and the seclusion. He turned around and blew cheery raspberries. They could tell that Acantia really liked the place. They pranced and stomped and hooted too. Pa tuned the viola with gusto and played into every corner of the building. The sounds moaned through the dry rot, shaking loose the mites, insects, worms, eggs, snakes, birds and gnawing through to something else which was resting in the damp throat of the house, back against the wet earth in which it was half buried.

Acantia prepared some soya bean salad for a cold lunch. She surveyed her lean and grimy children, smiling distractedly. 'You'll all be home-schooled here, true children of Nature. You will sit public examinations, and then go to Oxford University and study music or, if you wish, medicine. You'll be like Yehudi Menuhin. Marie Curie and Louis Pasteur! Sherlock Holmes! Pure minds! Inspirers and Discoverers. Heroes of the Twentieth Century. You'll put Australia on the map. We'll show 'em.'

The children spread through the strange building, swinging gingerly on the frayed ropes, testing for skeletons and other residents. Salt damp had spread like an enclosing hand from the dissolving walls against the rock face to the front of the dark hall. But it was late morning and the house was sunny and lovely.

Beate caught herself in the middle of a hoot and stopped. She walked outside and began to cry to herself. She leaned against a young radiata pine that stood at the head of a long row near the house, and turned and stared at the wreck that was to become their home. She was ten, and being the eldest and most responsible Houdini was becoming an impossible strain. Ursula ran up to her, tossing her lank blonde hair out of her eyes.

'Great, isn't it?'

Beate stared at her sister's ear. It was curved and sculpted, as if it were the cast, the negative of the head of a violin, a small vortex running into the mystery of Ursula's head. She calmed her breathing and hid her dismay in her clenched hands, crushed against the bark behind her back.

'It's a desert.'

'*Deserted!*' Ursula shrieked, and scampered away in a horse's gallop, her bony knees almost beating her chest. Her hair flicked and shone like a mane.

Beate stared at the house. It is a lost ark, she thought. The hall was surrounded by unpruned trees and then a sea of green-gold grasses, broken here and there with the red ugliness of half-hidden rusted car cabins, bonnets and chassis. Grass and rubbish dissolved into the bright and hostile bush perimeter, a uniform grey and silver barrier out of which the kombi had popped as if ejected. The trees glittered in the sunlight.

Beate was alone. She was assailed again with something she had been shutting out. She had been watching her changed mother for two sudden and shocking months and had had the occasional feeling that they had *fled* to this. It was not an adventure at all. It was the end. She could not understand it.

The thing in the back of her mind rolled towards her, lazy as a cat in the sun. It was a busy, after-concert scene, one of countless identical scenes. The children stiff and well dressed. The food. *Take one piece only and don't be the first.* Her father's eyes catching hers through a moving skein of long gold hair which for a moment veiled his face. The hair moved, flicked, and a woman she didn't know leaned in profile to whisper some word in Pa's ear. Pa's eyes were fixed on Beate's, trapped by her glance, his lips frozen in a kiss to that hair, his eyes begging. Then he turned away.

Beate was alone. She whispered to herself the words that tolled then in her heart with a kind of distinction and horror. I am the *eldest*. She didn't feel up to it. Ursula came sprinting by in a wheeling arc, head back and throwing gravel like an ecstatic puppy. Beate reached out a skinny arm and grabbed Ursula's collar, yanking viciously. Ursula tumbled and then leapt up, breathless, grinning. Beate was suddenly furious. She twisted Ursula's collar up tight and wrenched her sister's head close to her ear. Ursula grinned harder, choking, but her eyes shifted this way and that in bewilderment. Beate whispered hoarsely, 'I'm the eldest, and I have to do everything. Acantia is not . . . happy and I'm making that your job!'

Ursula went limp, wide-eyed and serious.

'Not happy?' she quavered.

Beate let her go and dropped her hands to her sides. She turned to the tree and began to sob. Ursula stood behind her for a while, then said softly and more than a little hopefully: '*You're* the one who's not happy.'

She leaned forward and punched the backs of Beate's knees so that her older sister slumped suddenly. Beate ignored her but stopped crying. It's hard to maintain a decorous sobbing when your sister has just scored on you in knee-knocking.

Ursula waited a moment for a better reaction and then walked away. She might have scored two points on Beate but her mood was still ruined.

Acantia held her hand reverently to the bark and cocked her head, as if listening. Ursula was impressed. Acantia listened to the voices of the spheres for a while, nodding her head now and then. Suddenly she gasped. 'The sadness of this place is to be redeemed!' She beamed at Ursula, 'And we are chosen to do it!' Ursula beamed back.

It was confirmed. They had a mission here and it was all *meant to be*. Ursula's doubts sank again into dreams and darkness and she charged about happily redeeming the land, pulling up weeds, collecting rubbish, planting seeds in the clay, and helping Acantia varnish the jarrah boards in the kitchen while Pa replaced the floor in the auditorium.

Acantia raced about in excitement, the brightness that comes with fevers glittering in her eyes.

'Children,' their mother said. 'If you want something hard enough, it comes to pass. If you want this house to be repaired and habitable, think only of that and before you know it, *Your Will Bedone*.'

The house had five corners, four useable rooms, three chimneys, two doors, one toilet and no plumbing. It also had a stage, auditorium and catacombs of tiny dank dressing- and props rooms built deep into a steep and slippery rock slope. It was a long and oddly shaped building, stone at the blind, buried end and brick and timber at the front. Part of it had once been a Temperance Institute and seemed to have been the last building standing of a tiny aborted bush colony, long forgotten. But there was much more. It had started as a two-roomed adobe settler's cottage with small windows and a steep roof. This was slipping down the hill off the side like a dead limb, no glass in its windows and its skeleton showing. Even destroyed, it preserved an oddly familiar air. Pa said that it must have been built by Germans. Acantia said that, shored up, it would make a good cow byre. On the other side was half a villa, and the verandah on that side had part of a terracotta mosaic on the floor and turned wood posts. The hall had been built without pulling down either of these once separate dwellings, and the extensions of the hall seemed to have cannibalised them. The remains of the villa were solid, but obviously unused for decades. The jarrah floors in the main house came from there. The hall proper was built of stone, but the main part of the house was built around it. Someone had converted it with four large front rooms and a return verandah.

The auditorium sat in the centre, a potential heartland. It was stinky, broken and festooned with webs, dust and mould. The stage was smashed and the floor had been chopped up with an axe. When Angus Bad had killed himself, some five years before, he had tried to take the house with him. Everything in it was broken.

Acantia said they could stage their own plays and concerts once they had repaired the floor.

The house was surrounded by a mass of European trees. A deodar cedar, a strawberry-rose apple tree and a twist willow were planted near one corner. Claret ash, a purple plum, a snowball, cherry plum, rhododendron, conker conifer, ivy, variegated cherry and other unnameable trees rubbed leaves and branches around the side of the house. As time passed these slow-growing giants competed with steady and silent violence for the ground and the light. (When the house was gone, burned in three minutes to a carious crater, the tangled and seething embrace of the trees loomed as one mass into the space it had left, filling it almost overnight. The giant apple tree hugged the scorched deodar, dripping with baked apples from its remote tips to the alcoholic mess around its horny trunk.)

Acantia and Pa's room, the kids' room, the music room and the kitchen were the only rooms with doors and which had decent floors. Two of them were at the front of the smashed-up auditorium, the other two at the sides.

When they cleaned the house up, polished the floor and put in the window, the jarrah glimmered here and there like red treasure under the streaming sunlight. Their oak table looked stark, solid and inviting, spread with a striped flannelette sheet and stacked with oranges and blue frosted plums. They had as yet no chairs so they all sat together on the front steps, eyeing their beautiful new home with quiet delight. Acantia was happy.

'Musicians, artists and poets,' she said. 'That's what you'll be. Just like Pa and me and your Uncle Lochie.' She sighed happily. 'No contaminants here! You'll be as pure as the Aborigines.'

The house had peculiar windows. Most rooms had none at all, or windows that looked in onto other rooms, rather than outside. It was an inward looking house. The windows increased the impression that the house knew something about itself and wasn't telling.

Acantia said it didn't matter. She would paint pictures of all the beautiful scenery around and they could look out through them. And she did. The children could look out, not just at the land and trees stretching up the hill, not just at the bush tracks leading away from their place, but at other countries. Sagans, Lucerne, Lake Constance, the Matterhorn, the Sisters and Mont Blanc, Engelberg and Hohenstaufen crags could all be seen from the windows of their house. After a while they forgot that they had the lights on all the time, remembering only when one guttered and spat and then plunged them and the luminous paintings into darkness.

THE ORCHARD

The blue-black forest furs the mountain like boar's bristles, echoing closer, nearer over the hidden brooks, hidden deer and other wonders until it winds like a buckled hunter's bugle call through the wind-coiled cherry trees, quince trees (they cannot see cherries or quinces) over the sea swirl of green, sonorous grasses (hiding the strawberries they once found) and out into the eye.

It is their own orchard in Germany unravelled from the paint tubes in Prussian blue and swirling helixes, made up of myriad sweeping streaks of greens and blues and cadmium yellow. It looks like a picture of music issuing from an old gramophone flower. Forest voices throbbing in one shouting chord through the throat of the orchard. This painting is from the epoch before Acantia developed her signature style. There are no broad horizontal brushstrokes, no firm vertical.

The Houdini children were advanced for their years. They knew their sums and read voraciously. They were all *phenomenally talented*, but in different ways. They were very proud of it. Beate the firstborn was the most clearly musical one. At ten she was already a prodigy. When she wasn't practising the violin, staring intensely into some inner space at ceiling level, she was usually singing to herself. But these days she sang little, and just eyed her parents, sometimes angrily, sometimes warily. It took a lot longer to reconcile Beate with Whispers than it did Ursula.

Beate tried to talk to Gotthilf on the third day as he was sitting on the sunny steps reading the dictionary. He was, after all, the next oldest, and should share the load with her.

'Did you know,' Gotthilf paused, looked up through his long straw-coloured fringe to secure Beate's gaze, then glanced again at the spot pinned by his forefinger, 'that *totalitarian* means "permitting no rival loyalties or parties"?'

'Yes,' Beate lied crossly.

Gotthilf loved words, and controlled conversations with her by knowing more words than she did. He could go into *Did-you-know* strings for hours.

'*Didjano Didjano*,' she chanted. 'Stop it. I want to talk to you. Do *you* know . . .?' She trailed off. What did she know?

'You just wanted to be concert queen,' Gotthilf said quietly.

'But the great world would have swallowed you up. Acantia said so. We left everything for *your* sake, Beate.'

Beate stared at him, wide-eyed. Then she ran. Gotthilf threw a handful of pebbles after her.

'It's true!' he screamed. 'Queenie! *Regina optima, planusque Gloria!*'

Gotthilf at that time probed the mysteries of the world with his fingertip. He lugged the Oxford around the yard, its spine ticking with the strain, his head bent down over it. He used the most peculiar words for the sake of being hard to understand. He'd say things like 'The moon has ameliorated the darkness'.

Over time, and with less and less contact with people from the outside world, Gotthilf's language had a slight influence on everyone's speech.

He was, when they moved to Whispers, only nine. He had the same leggy, knobbly build as Ursula, but already a perplexed, quick smile and the look of a boy hoarding love. He wasn't a show-off like Ursula. Show-offs have the resilience to take it or leave it. He had to stalk it, corner it, catch it and kill it to feel as though it was fully his. Both Pa and Acantia beat him more often than the other kids.

Gotthilf's huge dictionary was a kind of shield and a source of various kinds of power. The power of greater knowledge was only one. Words themselves led him out of Acantia's world and beyond her reach. But in this moment, this snapshot of Gotthilf at age nine, he still had to get Pa or Acantia to explain any word that was unsatisfactorily explained by his Oxford. For example:

'Rapine? That is when a man rips a woman's clothes off.'

There is a silence. The children shuffle and smile at each other. Beate smoothes her dress down and Ursula hitches her trousers up. Gotthilf, standing as always just behind Acantia's shoulder, whispers something in her ear.

'Yes, all of them.'

The children stare at her, dumb with horror at the picture she has conjured up. Acantia shudders involuntarily and pushes Lilo off her lap.

'Rape is a *terrible* thing. Food additives have a lot to answer for.'

Slowly Gotthilf was to piece together the outline of a world Acantia could not account for or explain. At nine he had just a hint, here or there, that Acantia's word was not to be believed if the Oxford said otherwise. He kept this knowledge to himself. It was not long before he stopped focusing on words that would impress others and began collecting words that impressed him, words that if used would get him hit more often. With these he could vent bitter little streams of unhappiness and spite. He sometimes crouched in his dirty shorts in the kitchen corner muttering and spitting a string of boneless vowels between his teeth, all his forbidden words, consonants removed. No one knew that what he was saying had any sense to it, and he began to get cuffed whenever he spoke indistinctly, because he sounded too much like a moron for Acantia's liking, and perhaps she sensed some latent power to his incantation. Malevolence is not tolerated in nine year olds in any case.

Gotthilf, like Ursula, didn't much mind the move, but, unlike Ursula, didn't see it as a huge adventure. As far as he could tell, it had been planned from before his birth. Everything had been. There was no point in getting excited. Just as he felt superior to Beate in his knowledge, he felt superior to Ursula in his disdain for enthusiasm. The twins, Helmut and Siegfried, seemed to him beneath contempt. Their interest in red trucks, yellow bulldozers and saying four times between them everything they had to comment on disgusted him. And Lilo, well she wasn't really a member of the family until she started walking and talking properly.

In fact Gotthilf's life had been unpredictable, tossed on sudden storms and major changes. He remembered their life before Germany, dimly, with its dusty back yard, passing goods train, Mr Clymo's horse, midmorning galahs and high washing line. He remembered the suddenness with which they had sold everything and rushed, dropping his teddy bear on the tarmac, to find their destiny in the Music of Europe. He remembered Beate's *talent* that later became Beate's *pride and arrogance*. The suddenness of Pa's concerts, their impromptu holidays, their wealth and mysterious pennilessness and wealth again. He knew that if he had said he didn't want to go somewhere they were going, his words would have sounded like a flutter of a passing bird's wings: sound without meaning or consequence. He was a boy who needed a carapace and an Oxford English Dictionary.

After several scares with red-bellied black snakes in the long grass, Acantia ordered Pa to slash all the grass in a hundred metre radius from the house and its trees. They discovered a tractor (and snake); an outside toilet with no cabin (and snake); a henhouse (and snake's nest); a ferret run (with wombat); an empty pond (plus snakes); and a rusty ladies' Bullock bicycle (no handlebars but plenty of redbacks). The place just got better and better, from the twins' points of view. Every night, that first spring, a fox wailed at the glorious stars.

Siegfried and Helmut talked incessantly about the activities of snakefoxes. They dressed as snakefoxes, with their shirts on their legs and their underpants on their heads. They demanded snakefox stories at night and, by agreement, arrived at all specifications of snakefoxes and their behaviour.

'Snakefoxes bite you,' Siegfried said.

'Snakefoxes bite you,' Helmut echoed softly to himself, thinking it over. Then he turned on Siegfried, 'No! Snakefoxes bite *you*!'

'No, Snakefoxes bite you.' Siegfried insisted.

Gotthilf smacked them both across the head, yelling, 'Say things only *once*!'

The twins howled in unison until Gotthilf was punished.

'Snakefoxes smack 'im better,' Helmut said to Gotthilf, who was nursing weals on his arms.

'Snakefoxes smack 'im better,' Siegfried said, nodding sagely, opening his eyes wide at Gotthilf.

'Snakefoxes smack 'im better,' Helmut said to Siegfried.

Siegfried nodded, turning to go. 'Snakefoxes smack . . .'

Gotthilf grabbed Siegfried's head like a ball, slamming one

hand over his little brother's mouth. He held on for thirty seconds, shaking in fury, roaring through gritted teeth.

Ursula was fascinated by both the living and the dead, and particularly the short transition in between. Dead animals filled her with sadness and pleasure. At night, curled in her pyjamas under the blankets, she imagined she was a highwayman's horse, mortally wounded with a bullet to the chest, gasping through the slow transition to death on a bed of gorse. (Beate found her little sister's death rattle intolerable.) Ursula taught herself taxidermy and probed flesh and skeletons with exploring fingers. Her mother said that this meant she was immune to grief.

Ursula was delighted that they were to live in the house of a suicide. She began the collective hunt for buried treasure. She secretly hunted for the suicide's vestiges. He might have left a baby or a small child lying about the place. If she found it first, it would be hers. If it was dead, well, she could get its skeleton.

She avoided finding Lilo, who always needed a nappy change and had a habit of finding Ursula. After nappy changing became Ursula's job, she decided a dead baby would be better than a live one.

In the kids' room, three double bunks were like galleons and a single bed floated in the middle like a life raft. It was not a high room: the top bunks were so close to the ceiling that a person couldn't sit upright. Eventually the kids punched a few small holes for ventilation, but a strange smell came down out of the ceiling space so, except for one, they stopped them up. The room had a small triangular window. Pa fixed a grid to the window so that the baby, who was then Lilo, wouldn't climb through and hurt herself by falling onto the verandah floor.

The music room, later the old music room, was the same size as the kids' room and directly opposite across the auditorium. It had an upright piano, floor-to-ceiling books on staggering shelves, four or five music stands and several gradations of violin and viola. The floor was powdered with resin dust. It originally had no window and was hung with beautiful paintings of Austria in winter. When the light broke they played in the dark. One year, Pa became infuriated with them playing wrong notes in the Emperor's Quartet and knocked a hole in one of the walls, letting in a jagged blast of sharp white light.

The kitchen was the largest room, other than the auditorium and the stage. It had an open-hearth fireplace big enough for three people to sit in, open through the wall to the auditorium. First thing in the morning it was still hot from the night before. Acantia cooked bolar roast, onions, potatoes and silverbeet in a top-hat pressure cooker stashed all day in a corner of the fire. If it worked, the roast was so good that it fell apart in onion-honeyed skeins and the potatoes were reddish orange toffee almost to the core. The onions disappeared altogether. When it didn't work, it was charcoal but they chewed on it anyway.

The fireplace was the only hot, dry place in the house in winter. All the walls oozed moisture and the sheets were damp. They huddled around the fire, steaming and contented, and it roared and flared welcomingly when they opened the door and walked in. Fire loved them and they loved it.

The kitchen had a low ceiling that Acantia papered with paintings done by the children. She gummed the backs, laid them over the broom and swept them over the marine blue.

The kitchen had a wooden floor with holes in the corners by the skirtings. At first they thought of rats but later they blamed the house itself. When the house was gone they found piles of molten cutlery, coins and ashen jewellery stashed away where the floorboards had coffined them.

The kitchen also had a real window; a huge expanse of glass, four foot by three.

Mr Tarsini was the Man in the Window. The Tarsinis were their neighbours over the years. They also had a family of six children, and had a baby to make it seven at about the same time as the Houdinis. The Tarsinis were as messy as the Houdinis, although they were much quieter. They were very similar but conducted their affairs in a more civilised fashion. They were three girls and four boys, all with the same names as the Houdinis and the same ages. At times they were ignored and at times watched avidly. Ursula, Siegfried and later Lilo were amused at first by their identical forms and mannerisms, and then, bit by bit, noted the differences. The Tarsinis' world was dimmer and the dirt didn't show. The dimensions of their house were bigger and the dimensions of their Pa smaller. They fitted into their world with less trouble than the Houdinis squeezed into theirs. They were theatrical when the Houdinis were serious. They were creatures of the night. The Houdini kids only ever saw the back of Acantia Tarsini's head and in turn Acantia Houdini always sat with her back to the window. She was, however, made conscious of the Tarsinis' antics by the attention they elicited from her own children, and she was increasingly annoyed by imbecilic behaviour directed at the window.

The game of sea warfare was played out in the kids' room in smothered explosions. Then, when everyone got tired, several raised tents of sheets glowed eerily long into the night. In the early years, the most intensely pursued pastime was sillytalk and the favourite story was the Three Billy Goats Gruff.

The punishment for being caught sillytalking was the same as for 'shit' or 'bloody': mouth washed out with soap. This made it all the more enticing. Beate and Gotthilf couldn't stand it but the rest of them could be reduced to hissing paroxysms of laughter squidged between their teeth and eyelids by the sound of Siegfried and Helmut sillytalking into the night.

'Bottom,' Helmut started, leaving the word hanging in the darkness. Silence. Then from the other bunk the retort,

'Pu-pul.'

'Shhhhhh,' Beate's bunk rocked and springs whined with her irritation.

The conversation died but the air was tense with many pricked ears.

Then . . .

'A-Aa.'

Siegfried snorted in agony and squeaked, 'Wee Wee Penis!'

Little snorts of laughter began popping and bubbling around the room. Helmut waited. Everyone got themselves under control and began drifting towards sleep, smiling. Then, into the still air:

'*Mister* Yewrine.'

The galleons whined and rocked. Mouths were stuffed with pillows as Acantia burst into the room with a blare of light.

Then . . .

. . . squeezed voiceless giggles . . .

'*Kss kss kss kss kss kss!*'

'Hey, *Mr*!'

'Shhhhh!'

'We'll shhhhhh if you tell the story.'

'Tell the story, Ursa, tell the story.'

THE THREE BILLY GOATS GRUFF

Once upon a time there were three billy goats, one little, one middling and one big. They lived in a field by a stream over which there was a bridge. On the other side of the river the grass was green and speckled with flowers. The tall trees gave shelter from the sun and rain. On their side the grass was dry and stalky, coarse and sparse, and they only got soya beans and wheatgerm for dinner. There was no shelter. They longed to cross over that bridge. But under the bridge there lived a troll who ate goats.

Gulp! Just like that . . .

The Three Billy Goats Gruff reigned in the kids' room that second summer. It then ticked away in the hearts of the children like a clock in a crocodile's belly.

Goats are courageous, Siegfried wrote, much later, in his goat diary.

They all played violin, viola or cello. They restored the auditorium and three little studios to deal with the cacophony. The house thrived on the discord and the heated competition for practice rooms. It looked like an ancient rat's nest with bears trying to fit in it.

By the time most of the children were teenagers, the place was littered with defunct half- and three-quarter size violins, broken bows, discarded strings. The floor around the good piano was thick and sticky with resin. Pa and Acantia spared no expense on musical instruments and once Ursula and Gotthilf were playing Mozart sonatas, they had instruments of fine make and exquisite tone: concert performance instruments. From six o'clock in the morning the house was filled with sound and fury, *Sturm und Drang*. Two pianos but few pianists, two cellos and cello players, numerous violins and two to three violin players, two viola players, one double bass player. A few of them dabbled in woodwind, brass and percussion.

They sang before meals. Acantia insisted on it. *Dona Nobis Pacem* and *Ehre Sei Gott* in four-part harmony. Siegfried quietly sang *Goat* for *Gott*.

Arno was born in the middle of the night. One night he wasn't there, and the next morning he was, all red and ugly and bundled in a clean white blanket no one had seen before. A doctor came round to see Acantia and told her to stop having babies at home. He came out of Acantia's room shaking his head.

'What sort of people are you?' he said in the kitchen to Pa, obviously cross. Pa shuffled, looked around and didn't answer. The doctor wiped a patch of the table with his hankie and had begun to write prescriptions when Acantia burst into the room in an unfamiliar new nightie, looking pale and small. Ursula had a sick feeling in her stomach. Acantia was crying.

'I know you! I know your kind! Get out!' She pointed a finger at the door with such sizzling expulsion in her eyes that most of the kids slunk out from various exits. The doctor sighed, handed Pa the prescriptions and walked towards the door.

Acantia snatched the prescriptions from Pa's hands. 'Toxins! He would try to get the child's own father to feed me toxins, oh yes!' She shredded them and threw the pieces at the doctor's back.

The doctor hesitated a moment, then kept going. 'I'll send the district nurse,' he called angrily as he got into his car.

Ursula watched him go, much cheered. *Don't bother sending your evil handmaiden, craven quack. We will make short shrift of her.* She swished her rapier. *Dispatched!*

After he had left, Acantia stood for a long time wrapped by Pa's huge arms. Gotthilf was the only one left in the room. Acantia's and Pa's faces were turned from him, closeted together in a soft humming space made by Pa's shoulders and her long dark hair. Gotthilf thought he should leave, but stood, blankly, soaking up the mystery of it. Acantia and Pa broke the spell, separating, going together to her room, returning to Gotthilf with the sleeping baby. He flicked a glance at each of them in turn and breathed out. He wasn't in trouble. The others trickled in and Pa showed them little Arno Zoroastre Houdini and his long fingers and delicate blue eyelids.

Arno, the quietest and the sweetest, child of Acantia's blue period, was the dreamer.

The kids' room served as sleeping space for all the children, a temporary measure that lasted several years. They fought over Arno, cuddled like a kitten or a hot water bottle in the bed of whoever could wheedle him with promises and scary torchlight to crawl in with them. Acantia hoped to repair some of the rooms under the stage but by the time the children were reaching their teenage years, they were too tall to stand up in them. The damp crept further forward year by year, slowly eating away anything that was rock or mortar under the timber beauty of the front of the house, while armies of white ants, spitting acid and leaking minute puffs of methane, rose steadily through the timbers from ancient caverns beneath the earth.

In winter the grass, the mud, the clothes, the people, the walls and the beds were cold. The fire, the cats and the fresh cow pats were warm. Everything was wet. They loved the fire, fought over the cats and stood barefoot in cow pats.

It was Gotthilf's job to find and cut the wood and Ursula and Siegfried's job to gather kindling. The kitchen was dank and miserable when the fire had no fuel or the wood was mean and wet. A steady breeze blew down and in from the auditorium. Gotthilf chopped piles of wood out in the drizzle under the big radiata pine. The chips flew, spattering through the air and landing with small wet sounds in the mud. He swung the axe with a dogged determination until he had chopped just enough to coax the fire through the day, and then came inside with a dripping armload of wood and his hair plastered to his forehead.

Acantia and Ursula stood on the verandah watching the goats. Venus stared balefully at Acantia from the shed. Acantia eyeballed her until the goat turned away, and then Acantia slowly shook her head.

'That goat does not like me,' she said to Ursula. 'But she does carry art around on her head.'

What is *that on that beautiful child's head? Oh, let me touch. My goodness gracious, horns! You are blessed, child, and will have a rare spirilli hornspan of five feet. Golden, too. Just like your hair. Remarkable! You must be very proud of your daughter, ma'am. She will have art wherever she goes.*

They had bought four goats when they moved into the house: Jupiter, Venus, Mars and Pluto. Jupiter had a spiralled, rippled horn-span of almost two metres. He had a long curly beard and looked like an ovine Father Christmas. He had grimy hair but was gentle, if aloof. Acantia said he was impotent because he didn't stink the way a billygoat should. Venus had a fine-boned, dished face framed by locks of white hair and a high brow divided in two for the twin arcs of her horns. These spiralled outward in a still, symmetrical image, rippled like tidal flats. She had bright golden eyes with mesmerising oblong pupils. She was wild, by reputation untameable. Ursula hung about her just out of jabbing reach. The wild goddess slowly began to tolerate her company but Ursula was never sure if Venus really befriended her. Blood and yellow lumps appeared in her milk and Venus died before there was time to find out. Her kids were hand-raised.

The children worked together burying Venus. They dragged her carcass down to the bottom paddock and began to dig a huge hole. Beate gathered flowers with solemnity and Siegfried stood holding herbs to put at her mouth. Helmut, Gotthilf and Ursula dug until they were standing in a hole up to their chests, heaving out the last shovels of earth. Lilo watched, squatting like a mottled frog in the long grass. They were all serious and sombre. Strains of a viola floated down from the house, falling like ash through the breeze.

The hole was ready. Gotthilf and Ursula dragged Venus over and toppled her in. Unbelievably, she seemed to have swelled. The hole looked tiny and legs and horns jutted out all over the place. They grabbed bits and tried to pull her out again but she was much too heavy. The great mass settled into the hole and barely moved with all of them tugging. Jupiter was staring at them all the while from the goats' paddock and they felt acutely embarrassed. Ursula jumped in on top of her and manipulated her head by the horns. She stuck the nose up in one corner and pressed the horn on the other side deep into the soft earth. Gotthilf and Beate wrestled with the stiffened limbs, loosening them, bending and wedging them into the sides of the hole. Gotthilf was crying in frustration. Beate shuddered.

'I think she's in.'

They looked down at her contorted form. As an afterthought they scattered the flowers and placed the herbs but after what they had done it seemed rather grotesque. With relief they shovelled in the earth around her and packed it down. They had filled it in before they realised that her belly swelled upward to slightly above ground level. They piled on the earth but it slithered off, revealing a plump mound of grimy locks. They wetted the earth into mud patties and packed them on. It did not look very satisfactory.

Gotthilf said hesitantly, 'I think we should jump on her a bit.'

It was a distasteful suggestion but they were not sure what else to do. He climbed gingerly onto the elastic mound and jiggled a little. Then he wailed, 'You all have to help!'

They piled on and began jumping up and down. Helmut giggled and set them all off. Just then from deep within the earth Venus gave a long, juicy fart. They roared and leapt in terror and then jumped on her with all their might, shrieking with laughter. She deflated bit by bit and settled into her grave.

They had to go down periodically and cover exposed bits. Venus rotted very publicly. When summer came the taut dry skin of the belly, hairless and hollow, could be beaten like a drum.

Not long after Venus died Jupiter jumped the fence and went feral. Occasionally he was seen leaping away with the wild goats out beyond the boundary fence. Mars and Pluto were then castrated and became pets for a while. Eventually they went to the butcher. They were useless and Mars had taken to headbutting. Despite Acantia's insistence on keeping only nannies, the goat herd grew and Acantia had to buy a stinky billy to stop the uninvited bachelors getting birthday cake for free.

Pa played his viola nine hours a day. The viola repertoire structured their days. If the children ever thought about it, they liked it. Pa said a lot about himself and them on the viola. They were proud of him, for he had been a great player in the outside world, in the time before they moved back to Australia.

THE PRINCESS AND THE VIOLA PLAYER

Once, long long ago in a time long gone before, there was a musician, a viola player. He could play the sun from behind the clouds, the snowflakes into a dance, the night into day. His viola sang a song that only people can understand: he made them happy that they were sad. He was the most famous a viola player can be and everyone in all the countries wanted him to play to them so they could be happy that they were human beings, not dogs or goats or horses. They gave him money, and flowers and beautiful instruments, and they recorded his playing so they could take a little bit home with them to have with dinner. But the viola player was so lonely that he could not be happy that he was sad, no matter how beautifully he played.

Then one day he met a dark and lovely princess with a mouth like a sword, and he ran away with her to live in secret. The people were left to their sadness and their records.

He had escaped.

That was the story Ursula told.

Acantia was very beautiful in old photos. She was very beautiful in hand-me-down memories.

One of Acantia's early paintings was a very small board squidged all over with squirts straight from the tube. It was of an old tree but that was clear only from a distance. It was like a close-up of every insect's life cycle speeded up. It was hot with colour. The trunk was scored with a stroke of cadmium yellow over a seething charcoal, Prussian blue and red trunk. They all loved it when very young, partly because it contained a menagerie of weird three-dimensional creatures who invited eye contact and initiated furtive conversations.

'Oi. Pssst. You there in your Papa's pyjamas.'

At the end of the cadmium streak was a fat yellow duckling with a looped tail which all the children could see, but the painting also held private secrets for select viewers. There was a drunk-looking orange squirrel with one very long finger. There was something with its eye up against a hole in the trunk, looking out at them. It was silly and mysterious. It was comforting to look at again and again. It was a painting they grew out of but always felt sentimental about. It was Acantia's only cosy painting, a kids' painting. It reminded the children of Pa.

Pa was very tall. He was tawny and downy, just like his children. He was seven foot or more and built like a bear. He had grown from a particularly straight and beautiful sapling. Photos of him when he was courting Acantia show a young, godlike being, all planes and shadows, tall and lean, with the awkward grace of a shy man hidden inside a perfect body. His eyes, somehow both resigned and desiring, longed for sex and serenity—in that order. In one photo he is bracing himself against a giant monolith that is perched precariously on another. His arms are wrapped around it, long fingers outspread, his body arched backward and pressed to the rock, straining muscles running down his thigh and leg. His cheek lies against the granite, the smooth skin pressed into the coarse grain. His teeth are white and his eyes laughing for the unknown young Acantia behind the lens.

He had some impressive snorts, farts, goat-scaring noises and burps. When he burped at the table, he said, '*Scoozi*.'

So did they.

Pa's hands, like his body, were huge. They wrapped around the thin, tiger-eye neck of the viola like the maw of a Rottweiler around a stick. Then they danced, each finger making room for the other at the precise point, the precise moment, the only moment, to give off the pure, painful sound. His fingers each walked a taut highwire, stretched over a chasm of silence.

Pa stood playing viola in front of a painting of Pa playing the viola. His brow worked and furrowed, and his ears waggled. His torso tossed about like a tree in a storm. The painting is a frozen midpoint that somehow manages to make the same movements. Churning spirals of purple and grey swirl around the still furrowed brow and a garishly, grotesquely twisted instrument. Pa's ears and brow and body sometimes touched exactly that moment, but his instrument stayed pristine and symmetrical, never going down the vortex of such timber-splitting torsion.

'Isn't it strange that Pa doesn't have a real name?' Ursula asked Beate.

'Of course he has a real name. He just doesn't need it any more because he's Pa.'

'But who was Pa?'

'A Hartmut Houdini, the violist.'

'No one's a violist,' Ursula spat it out crossly. 'That's what he does, not what he is. Who was he when he was a boy, when he was as old as me?'

'I don't know. I wasn't there.' Beate, too, was annoyed. She intended to be a violist.

'Do you think he played . . .'

'Pa can play *anything, anytime*. Listen. He's playing now.'

'. . . games?' Ursula sighed. Pa was very playful. She knew he would have played games. What she really wanted to know was whether or not he had anything happening inside his head, now or in the past. Ursula couldn't imagine Pa as a real grown-up. But she couldn't imagine him being young like her either. What was Pa when he was alone and had no instrument and no family, no discord to soften, no frayed tempers to settle, no strings to tune? She had no idea. He might as well have been a hollow log, a disused double bass.

She knew him as little as she knew Acantia. She knew exactly what they would do or say, just as when Pa's bow was poised above the open strings of the viola, she knew exactly what sound was coming. But what they thought or desired was masked. How was it that one could have such hidden parents?

She wandered outside into the sunlight and away from the house. She knew that, a few metres behind her, Lilo would be hovering, her fierce face beaming with love and desire. Ursula trailed Lilo like a cape. She didn't need to look, any more than Lilo needed to be told that Ursula liked being shadowed. Ursula sighed, knowing the little face would be puckering in sympathy. Then she spun and pounced, punching her sister hard in the stomach and churning the gravel as she ran. Lilo tore after her, shrieking with a rage close to joy.

Lilo was like a budgerigar: convinced she was the same size or larger than anything she met. She was fierce about everything. She was fierce about art. She didn't need paint. Mud and blood would do. Acantia almost never beat Lilo.

crescendo

Beate turned thirteen first. Pa moved out of Acantia's room into the corner of the auditorium. The smell in Acantia's room changed from a heady fug to something colder. Helmut and Siegfried moved to camp in the old music room, and the galleons were dismantled. Beate's house was built, and Beate and Gotthilf moved into it. Arno slept in his own bed in the kids' room, the head of a long-haired doll clutched in his fist. Lilo and Ursula shared the room with him. Lilo's bed stood over a nest made of paper and small pieces of the body and limbs of the same doll.

Acantia cried through the night instead of sleeping but her children only twitched and whimpered like puppies and licked her gently in their dreams. Pa snored in the corner of the auditorium with a dying fall reverberating in the heart of the house.

The house sighed into the dark air, making a smiling sound.

Pa didn't move back into Acantia's room until after the children left home.

A slow tragedy was taking place in Pa's hands. Pa was always home now and rarely rang Odo Schmelzle, his agent. There were no more concerts after they left the great world. These days Pa practised as though preparing for one all the time. The children weren't allowed to interrupt when Pa played, and so he was out of reach for nine hours a day. But they could hear him, always. His slow decline kept tempo with their fading certainties.

Pa's joints thickened and ached prematurely. He played harder to ease their stiffness, but they fought him, and his knuckles tried to huddle together like old peasants with their backs to the cold. When the sweet, tense, crying of the viola became rougher year by year, the changed sounds crept up on the children so stealthily that most of them didn't notice until they had left home and begun to listen to other viola players.

The influence of the house extended to the borders of Acantia's property and sometimes beyond. Fences sagged, fence posts rotted and vanished into the earth. Gardens were aborted half grown and abandoned to weeds and drought. Whisperweed, blackberry and

African daisy marched inexorably over the fields, closing in year by year; and one by one the apple trees in the orchard were smothered and died. Radiata pines thrust their soft points through the clay, thickened and burst into full needle armour to march upwards and outwards, claiming earth and sky. The stringybarks were beaten back to the bush perimeter and, over the years, were invaded and shadowed by the taller pines. Animals developed chronic lamenesses and cats died giving birth. The young white cow, Radha, died of milk fever and a man came and chopped her up with an axe. From the house the children couldn't see the body or the man. They could only see the axe appear and disappear behind the shoulder of the hill.

Goats' hooves lengthened and curled. Bouts of ringworm predated their stalky hair and raised weals on the children's forearms, which were splashed purple with gentian violet. Not long after Beate turned thirteen, she was struck down with boils. Great pustules grew and erupted, leaving permanent scars like craters or bullet holes in her smooth limbs.

A row of seven radiata pines divided the goats' paddock from the front paddock. The tallest shadowed the house, threatening the apple and the deodar at dusk. Acantia said that each tree represented one of the children, from oldest to youngest. Gotthilf hung a swing from the second tree, and broke his arm using it. The third tree, Ursula, was both crooked and stunted, too small for a swing or anything else. Useless. It had needles of a darker green and more thickly clumped form. Deviant, it said. Siegfried's tree had a magpie nest in it and, every spring, Ursula wished that she had been born fifth and was the one blessed with dive-bombing champions. Later Count Ugolini was to say that the seven trees should be *chopped down and chopped up*. They were too close to the house. They were a fire hazard in the driest state of the driest continent. Siegfried carved his initials into the knobbled trunk of the fifth tree. He said his tree wasn't him, but was his, and that he'd do with it what he wished, when the time came. Helmut tried to build a cubby in the lower branches of the fourth, but the tree ditched it and him into the mud below.

Neither Lilo nor, later, Arno paid the trees any attention. They were both babies of Whispers, and gravitated to the stringybarks and the bush.

Pine wood spat violently from the fireplace.

The old fort headquarters, the caravans Acantia had bought as spare bedrooms and the hovels the children built as escapes melted away and left only the rusting metal chassis and unidentifiable ruins littering the property in odd corners. The Houdinis were not even hobby farmers, and everything rotted or wilted away after a brief season of fanatical attention and enthusiasm. Vestiges of projects redolent with faded passion lay all about: a row of dying bottlebrushes; the whisperweed-choked orchard; the pit, later cow grave, that was to have been a swimming pool. Whispers gradually became one of those farms that look uninhabited; farms that look as though something sad has happened and people have walked away taking nothing with them.

Beate had begun to go into the city for violin ensemble and concerts and became, as the rest termed it, *urty p'turty*. She washed herself all over. She was embarrassed by her family in public. She secretly bought deodorant. She masked her siblings' seeping, all-permeating stench with cheap perfume.

Beate's house was supposed to give Beate space to practise, privacy in which to dress and undress, now that she had breasts, as well as the necessary independence and separation from parents that is only to be expected from a thirteen-year-old.

The new house was built by Joe, Burt and Terry. Joe was the boss and smiled a lot. Burt stank of smoke and Terry never wore his shirt, even when he was eating lunch. They all called Ursula 'Love' and Gotthilf 'Mate'. Ursula and Gotthilf tried to help as much as possible and had to be called away from the building site twenty times a day. Acantia called both of them 'nuisances'.

Joe, Terry and Burt had to build the house under constant surveillance from the staring, slack-jawed children. Only Ursula and Gotthilf would respond to conversation and chin-chucking. Beate stayed aloof, having been told about men and not talking to them, and the younger kids just stared harder and closed their mouths briefly when addressed directly.

Burt was their favourite.

'G'day, mate, how they hanging?' Burt would say to Gotthilf.

'Low, loose and fulla juice!' Gotthilf would shriek in delight.

'How's my girlfriend?' he'd ask Ursula, winking a bright blue eye in an expanse of copper skin.

'Good, Burt,' she'd say, beaming, looking quickly over her shoulder to check where Acantia was. 'Gimme five!'

And Burt would slap his big, calloused, smoke-smelling hand to hers.

The day the men piled into their pick-up and roared up the drive for the last time, three arms waving, Ursula felt a weight come down on her chest, despite the magically new, paint-smelling house they left behind.

Beate's house was a three room timber frame on stilts, facing the house from a few metres away. Almost all its windows also faced the house, giving it a yearning, leggy, baby-bird look. A path made of concrete blocks passed from the front door of the house, between the apple and the deodar with a half-playful curve, to the front door of Beate's house. From the kitchen, you could see even the light of a match struck in Beate's house, so there was no cheating curfew.

Gotthilf went with Beate to the new house, as a brother should. But he was evicted after a month for messiness and settled into a caravan that Pa parked just outside Beate's bedroom window.

The only book Beate took with her into her adolescence and into the new house was a few fragments of ***The Tomten***. Beate would be going home one day, and the winter would end.

In the deepest winter, when the farmhouse lies sealed away in the valley by snow drifts, and the moonlight plays over the buried fences and the eiderdown fields, the Tomten visits, leaving deep, blue-shadowed tracks in the expanses of snow. The pockmarks of his trail stretch across the glittering fields, then travel between the stark buildings in their thick white blankets, past the machinery and tools leaning each with icing along their lengths, past the tractor with its spokes dusted white and the apple crates highlighted on each slat with fine white thread. Alles schweiget. *The tracks enter the barn where all the animals are sleeping, dreaming of spring. To the goats he speaks in a language only goats can understand:*

Soon there will be ixodia for you to eat.

The tracks leave the barn and go under the white brow of the sleeping house, deep into the shadows. Wet pools from soft felt boots track across the wooden floor of the verandah. They cross the snow-buried path right up to Beate's window, where they stop. That is where he sings a song that only sleeping young violinists can hear:

Spring is coming.

Acantia's face was lovely, caught in the morning light streaming across the bed. Ursula held her breath, her heart twisting with longing. Acantia turned and patted the bed beside her, and Ursula leapt to sit there, straight and glowing. Acantia smiled at her and stroked the hair out of Ursula's eyes, and with that touch on her brow, Ursula was transformed, incarnated.

'Oh, Ursa,' Acantia said softly. 'We never think of you! What would you like *most* in the whole world?'

Ursula's delight drained out of her and her smile stiffened to a mask of brightness. More than anything in the world she wanted a horse. But what would Acantia want her to be wanting? Her mind riffled in a panic for something. She said the first thing that she could think of.

'Trumpet lessons,' she breathed, hoping her voice sounded rapturous. The clarion, golden choice.

Acantia was so proud of her. It was the right choice.

Ursula liked her trumpet very much, just not the sound it made. She practised a lot of silent trumpet, carrying the instrument as an accessory when riding her imaginary horse.

Eventually it was confiscated and the lessons with Pa cancelled.

The Houdinis rigged up outfits from Salvation Army excursions and hand-me-downs of great lineage. Always a decade off centre and a few degrees off colour, they looked like visitors from somewhere else, a land where the sun doesn't shine. White was grey, red was brown or smoky flesh-coloured, black was brown, but a different brown from the formerly blue or green. The children didn't care but, as they got older, they yearned for nice, normal underpants. They shared an underpants drawer in the central built-in cupboard of the house. They hoarded a collection of reasonable looking ones filched when dry from the line and stretched them out as long as possible. Ursula could make one pair last three weeks before the crustiness was too irritating.

The children didn't care about being different. They were even proud of it until one by one they turned thirteen and wondered if all the things that made them distinctive really made them better than other people.

The misery of winter lifted with the onset of cold and shining days. In the spring whatever it was that was malevolent in the house was mostly quiescent. The sunlight sang, the trees glittered, the goats became fat, and a burnished copper glow radiated from the cow's sleek body. The children played in the bush or around the house, freed of school by midday, sap running riot in their veins. Acantia sat in the sun on the stairs of Beate's house, shredding the distant neighbours and smiling at Gotthilf's jokes. Breezes ruffled the brindled paddocks; the swelling seedheads stretched as far as the horizon hills and the bush border. The world looked wide, bounteous and delicious.

The children wove cubby houses and Secret Spots with swathes of broom, bacon-and-egg, witches hut tendrils and gum tree bark, weaving window casements and flax floors. The bushland was filled with these strange children's nests. Each had a small clearing and, for a little while, a crisp, civilised air. The thatching never worked. They leaked and disintegrated in the span of a season.

'My Secret Spot is dry in the winter and so warm you would think it had a fireplace.' No one had been able to find Helmut's Secret Spot, not even Siegfried. He shared his technique generously but would never disclose the location. He went around with a Secret Spot smile which everyone was meant to see and which drove everyone wild. They took turns tailing him but he just smiled.

'Just bend some sheets of iron and then cover it all with weaving and then cover that with mud. Then plant stuff on it, and if you give it a narrow entrance tunnel, no one will ever be able to tell.'

'It would sound hollow,' Ursula murmured.

The children ranged through the bush stamping on mounds and listening. Helmut just smiled.

'Just chop down some saplings and bend them into a ball and weave them with broom and then grow witches hut over it and no one will ever find it.'

The children poked witches huts with broomsticks.

Helmut smiled from his Secret Spot. The trick was if you made no mark you could not be found and your Secret Spot could be anywhere. But he was giving himself ideas and dreamed of building—really building—a hidden teepee, a hut, a refuge.

They rarely had visitors and weren't very good at the social graces. Once the Jehovah's Witnesses made it through the clay cutting and the overgrown bush track to knock a little nervously at the door, staring at the huge ruined fascia lying half buried in the garden between the two houses, reading the flaking Romanesque letters: 'omen's Temperance Institute'. Helmut and the younger kids gathered at the door. He was the oldest one home. He waited, silent. They knocked again.

'Who's that trip-trapping over my bridge?' he called out firmly.

They didn't answer. He didn't open the door and they left.

The house was a remote castle, well fortified with sundry discomforts, overeager, almost canine, hospitality and bad table manners. Relatives from overseas usually visited for an hour or during daylight. Sibylla and Grog, however, came to stay. They had been friends of Acantia and Pa when the Houdinis lived in Germany, long ago.

When Sibylla and Grog arrived, everything changed. They got Beate's house and the first thing they did was ban the kids from wandering in. This was the first sign of an inveterate unfriendliness. Grog frowned all the time and Sibylla smiled all the time, even when she was being unfriendly. The main house's toilet broke down.

However, Sibylla befriended Ursula after a while and together they built a garden. It had rows of herbs and vegetables and Rapunzel lettuces. It was out of sight and earshot of the house.

Sibylla, smiling all the while, told Ursula that Acantia knew nothing about the harmony of the spheres and surrendering to true destiny. Sibylla was a good gardener but clearly did not know Acantia very well.

Sibylla and Grog were leaving: the kombi was piled up with their stuff and they had airplane tickets. The day before there had been much shouting behind closed doors and the children had slunk off into the bush until it was over. Now Pa and Acantia were silent and Grog was very cold to them. The same day, Acantia rushed down to the garden and ripped everything up. She trampled the seed beds like a rhinoceros stamping out a fire. Ursula was enraged beyond caution. Acantia said that if Ursula wasn't careful she would turn out just like Sibylla.

Ursula said she hoped so. At least Sibylla knew how to be gentle and smile and build a garden.

Beate told Ursula a few years later that Sibylla had tried to swap Grog for Pa. Ursula wished then that she had helped Acantia to destroy the garden. She was so burdened by her former loyalty to Sibylla that she pretended to herself that sabotage had been her purpose all along.

Count Antonio Ugolini was the second friend of the Houdinis. When Count Ugolini came no one saw him as anything other than he seemed: a dispossessed multi-millionaire aristocrat with a yacht and a Stradivarius.

He appeared one day, calm and quiet, stepping out of his car and through the kitchen window into the house as if there was nothing strange at all about that. The door had been ripped off its hinges and nailed shut since the day Sibylla and Grog left, and the window was also still broken. Acantia was acutely embarrassed but struck by his breeding and aplomb. She had everything repaired before his next visit. From then on Count Ugolini called on them periodically, sat in apparent exhaustion in the *pride of the house*, the beautiful polished wood auditorium, and spoke quietly of his noble lineage and his suffering at the hands of his depraved family. Apart from the Stradivarius, he also loved collectable musicians.

He was a short, stocky man with a languid, suffering air. He had a lot of black bristles and big ears. He had a glutinous, honeyed voice. He claimed to be the heir to parts of Italy and Hungary, past and present, but was on the run from a senile father who refused to die and was trying to obliterate his gifted and mistreated son. Count Ugolini played violin, talked casually about the Stradivarius (stolen back from the long list of robbers who had stolen it from his great grandfather), was an artist and a sensitive soul who, more by luck than inherent resilience, had thus far escaped with his life.

Acantia loved Count Ugolini. Count Ugolini appeared to despise her, which increased her conviction of his superiority. Count Ugolini loved Pa. He even, late one night on his yacht, made a pass at him. Pa didn't notice and relayed the incident under the heading of jolly fellows having fun in a manly way. Many years later, when the house burned down, Count Ugolini sent Pa a mini-grand piano as a present.

Acantia and Pa, having known the count for some time, trusted him as if they knew every recess of his soul. They wanted their children to spend time with such a powerful, cultured and gifted individual.

'I am like the Conte de Monte Cristo,' Count Ugolini said. His long white fingers curled and uncurled around his fat knee. Ursula stared at his hands. They were much whiter and softer than her own. Her hands were brown and grimy. Where the cow's teat bedded in the firm muscle between her thumb and forefinger her skin was pink and honey gold. But over the backs of her palms and along each finger stretched a caul of ingrown dirt. She stared at her fingernails and cuticles and felt her calluses with each of her thumbs. For a moment she looked like Struwelpeter. She popped her thumbs out. Her thumbs were possibly cleaner than all the rest of her, pressed daily deep into the milk-slicked udder. The princesses bathed in milk, she thought, looking with casual affection at them. She glanced back to the Count's thumbs, fascinated by their bloodlessness. The Count continued in his modulated, sweet voice:

'I am exiled to a terrible prison, but I too have found great treasure.' He bent the beam of his eye down to Acantia and Pa, taking in the whole family in soft, misty focus. Pa was trying to look literary. Acantia was looking dreamy, even beautiful. The Count paused, facing the open door, watching Helmut, Siegfried and Lilo chasing each other outside. He sighed.

'You are most fortunate. Precious, precious children. I will never have a family. Too dangerous.'

Acantia wrung her hands in genuine distress.

'No! No. Don't say that. Things change. Let me read your palm for you!'

His hands shrank from Acantia's touch, disappearing into themselves. His closed hands looked like punched pieces of dough.

Ursula disliked the Count then, out of loyalty to Acantia. Ursula was eleven and she wondered what Acantia had that Count Ugolini would shrink from her.

Aborigines were the pitiful losers of the great race. As were the Italians, Balts, Greeks and Asians. Getting Australia was a race. White Northern Europeans won it, proving that they were faster, smarter and more evolved than those who came later. This win gave them the right to do what they liked. When Ursula said that then the

Aborigines really won, Acantia said they were passive not active inheritors of the land and so not in the race at all, in fact more like ethereal beings who suffered for being on a higher spiritual plane but in a much lower human form. Later Acantia found out that the Chinese discovered Australia years before the Europeans and didn't bother colonising it or messing with Aboriginal culture and she went quiet on the great race. But she couldn't get away from talking about Aborigines. Ursula came to accept that being Australian meant she was connected to and defined by these unseen fellows, Australians too but as shadowy and elusive as angels or dreams.

Underneath, Acantia despised white Australians, hated and feared more recent immigrant Australians, and was repelled by every Aborigine she saw. Nonetheless she yearned for something in her idea of tribal life and for one summer made the children form totems, improve javelin skills and get almost all over tans.

She threw in the whole notion of being Australian when a Saturday *Age* rode into Whispers on the back of a lettuce.

'Can you believe it! They have sunk so low. They've become materialistic. They want a different flag, and *land rights*!' Tribal life was over. She made the children become Spartans.

'Australia has no depth, no history,' she said, to get back at the Aborigines. 'That's why it has no art, no music and no literature. Young, silly, weak, corrupt. Look at this talk about letting in the Vietnamese. How will it ever get Culture with such a mish-mash?'

In the early years at Whispers, school started at 6.00 am with Instrument Practice. Then Animal Husbandry. Then there was a break for Breakfast and Song, then Home Skills (cleaning up ready for classes). At 8.45 some Physical Education and Eurhythmy, then at 9.00, The Three Rs. Acantia could do long multiplication and long division in her head and had beautiful penmanship. Both had elements of magic and secret powers. The children were enthralled.

At 10.45 they broke for some more Physical Education (usually a sprint up to the top dam and back, then some stretches). Then on alternate days they had History and Culture, or Science classes. Pa taught them European History, German Language and Culture; Acantia taught them the British Empire and Sums. Acantia took Science. Then they had lunch, and were free to paint, draw, sculpt, play with the microscopes, make music or musical instruments or garden until whenever they liked. Any time after 3.30 they were free either to continue whatever they had got engrossed in, or to run off into the bush or wherever and read or play. On clear summer nights they did Astronomy and Stellar Navigation. Other than the early start and caring for the animals in midwinter, Ursula loved all of it.

Occasionally Acantia checked up on what their contemporaries would be learning, and taught them those things too. But she had a tendency to ridicule anything that was foreign to her, and Ursula grew up with the impression that sets and calculus were a bit silly and Australian history negligible. New ideas and anything to do with politics were met with derision.

'Feminism, pah! Poor things just don't know how to be real women. Broken homes behind them and ahead of them. No-hopers.'

'People just aren't equal, so why they want to pretend they are, I don't know. Not everyone can be an artist, now, can they? Or a mathematician. Toxins on the brains, that Whitlam lot. Communists.'

'Multiculturalism! What will they think of next! What culture? They haven't got one, let alone many. More like Muddyculturalism.'

But the Houdinis did grow up with a bare bones sketch of contemporary Australia and reluctantly, slowly, learned not to trust Acantia's knowledge of everything. They instinctively knew, especially after reaching puberty, that she was afraid and that these views were bravado.

The man in the cream hat and the safari suit was there again. He stood in the clay cutting at the bush perimeter, staring down at them. He had been there the week before but because he had gone away, they had forgotten. Now he was back and somehow his presence seemed to cast a shadow over them and they couldn't play and shriek as before. They began watching the watcher, first out of the corners of their eyes and in little looks cast at each other, then they just stood around and watched back. The man in the cream hat and the safari suit was quite a distance away, so they couldn't make out his face. He lifted one foot onto the embankment and looked as though he was tying a shoelace. Then he straightened, shaded his eyes with his palm held in front of the brim of his hat and stared down at them. He took the stick he held in the crook of his arm and swished it. Then he strode straight down the bush track towards them. The children scattered.

Acantia met him ahead of Beate, Gotthilf and Ursula. The rest stayed in hiding. Pa was practising and hadn't noticed yet.

'Hello, what do you want, can I help you?' Acantia was shaken and couldn't quite be polite.

'Madam, could you please tell me, how many children do you have?'

Acantia looked hunted, and even the big kids huddled a little behind her. Lilo crept up and held onto Ursula's trousers.

'Madam, we have written to you on numerous occasions, with no response. It is illegal for school-age children to not attend school.'

'They attend school here,' Acantia said stiffly.

'Where?' The inspector looked around deliberately and returned his rather popped blue eyes to Acantia's face. He rocked back on his heels once, then forward, and straightened. Then he suddenly switched his attention to Gotthilf.

'Young man, how many brothers and sisters do you have?'

'Three . . . fo . . . four,' Gotthilf stuttered, frantically trying to work out who Acantia would be able to bear to part with.

The man in the safari suit smiled an unfriendly smile at Acantia, who stood stiff and white.

'And you, little missy?' he asked Lilo. 'How many siblings have you got?'

'Just me,' said Lilo, expansively.

'Well well well,' the school inspector said. 'I counted seven, s-e-v-e-n. And you say they go to school!'

Pa appeared on the verandah, waved his viola, saw Acantia's face, and said, 'We don't need encyclopaedias, thank you very much.'

The school inspector glanced up at him and smiled again. Then he turned his back and as he walked away he said, 'Make sure they are in school next week.'

'They are in school now, and what a mighty lesson they have learned!' Acantia suddenly screamed. 'The rudeness!'

That evening, as everyone sat around the table, the shadow the man cast from the hill had not lifted. Acantia strode up and down the kitchen, turning and turning, gasping. She stopped and stared at them, her eyes shining with tears.

'We are surrounded by PREDATORS!'

They didn't go to school. The education department sent a psychologist in a pale green Kingswood. He appeared through the clay cutting, slipping smoothly and easily along the bush track to the front porch entrance. There he sat for a moment, rustling his papers with his head down, perched behind a low burble of fine machinery. Then he got out and smiled brightly at Acantia. He had slightly long hair, square-rimmed glasses and tight trousers.

'Hello,' he said, extending a hand with silver jewellery on it. 'I'm Dr Driscoll.'

The children were stunned but Acantia just looked resigned and angry.

Dr Driscoll was nice and had a good fun day with the kids. The younger children showed him some of the abandoned Secret Spots and none of the current ones, although they told him that because he was nice they would have liked to and gave him lots of clues.

They enjoyed the tests he gave them and he told them they were fabulous children and that Acantia and Pa had done a marvellous job. When he asked Ursula, after her test, if she would like to go to real school, a special school for really special people, she cried. She thought probably she should cry at that point but she was still not sure why she did. She just liked Dr Driscoll and was overwrought by his likeableness. She was overcome by having been called special.

When the psychologist gave his report, Acantia relaxed and said all would be well. Then the education department accused her and Pa of harbouring geniuses and demanded that these fugitive intellects be returned to the state.

Acantia fought but one by one the children had to go to school. Beate was safe at sixteen, almost missing from the daily life of the family, for she practised violin eight hours a day.

She gave them Gotthilf first. She absolutely refused special school.

'What, so they can pretend it was their sick system that made these children what they are?'

Gotthilf, aged fourteen, went to Berg Area High, a local school situated on the slopes of the mountain that gave Toggenberg its name.

Gotthilf began his school career by picking fights with all the Aboriginal kids, jealous of their higher spiritual plane. He got thrashed about ten times in three days before he changed his attitude to Aboriginal boys. They, like the dictionary, clearly possessed a world of their own beyond his knowledge.

He couldn't leave them alone. He followed them, slinking

along in the bush, sauntering close to walls, looking in other directions disingenuously, or pretending to read the pocket dictionary he now carried. Occasionally they chased him, but in this one thing he excelled: he was a faster and wilier runner than any kid in school. Then they ignored him, and he became their shadow, his eyes, even in class, sliding to their dark faces and staying glued there. They beat him up mercilessly whenever they managed to catch him, but this increased his complicated yearning and respect. The other children also beat him up or held his head down the toilet whenever they could. Abo lover and Boong bonkers, they called him, but Gotthilf barely heard and developed no respect for them no matter how much they beat him.

Eventually he managed to lure Trevor into his world using a mixture of whistles and big words as bait.

'Columnar!' he shouted from the stands, skinny arm raised in salute, and then whistled with four fingers wedged in his mouth, as Trevor was playing football.

Then he hissed, 'Tachycardia,' in breathless excitement from the bushes behind the science block and Trevor pounced on him. Gotthilf smiled in delight and terror. Held up by the shirt front in Trevor's fist, he whispered, 'Gotya!' and put his finger gently in the red mouth of Trevor's dragon tattoo. Trevor beat him up.

Ursula was looking for a Secret Spot. She wanted one that was better and braver and more secret than Helmut's, which no one had been able to find. She went exploring in the deserted bowels of the house, half hoping still to find a skeleton of a baby. She would put it in her museum, properly labelled. This part was buried away from the mind and from daily life. It was a catacomb, a theatre of strangeness. She wormed her way through the low, gloomy doorways into the rooms entombed in darkness and damp. She sat in one of the dank, lightless rooms that backed straight into the hillside. It was piled up with invisible unidentifiable rubbish, filled with anything that could be surrendered to a slow demolition. She closed her eyes and breathed in the sweet acid smell of rock-eating water, the smell of decades of slow digestive acids and urine. She was deep in the stomach of the hillside, smelling its hunger and its insatiability. No matter what happened, it was clear that the house would not be surviving. It might rage but it was being eaten, slowly and surely, from within. The pockmarked, cratered wall behind her whispered wetly as her back pressed against the shards of paint and plaster. The ice cold of the underground seeped into her. She could barely hear the viola. It penetrated as a whisper-thin tonal wail, somehow itself sinister. She was the queen of darkness, reaching out with her fingers to destroy all. She spread her arms and paused, trying to think of a chant.

'Oooooooooh. Ooooooooh?'

Each howl fell stillborn into the tiny room. The feebleness of the sound scared her and she trailed off to silence, listening. The small darkness of her mind was a tiny nut and she felt suddenly as though it was being watched. Her eyes flew open and something rushed up, electric and excited at her permeability. The darkness leapt down her throat and bored out her eyes. She stumbled blindly for the door, hands outstretched. As she scrambled against invisible rusty tricycles, treading on decapitated dolls and broken toys, the wall behind her ran with fluid whispers and tiny flour bomb explosions as lumps of plaster, fragments and flakes fell or slid to the floor. When she tumbled out into the daylight she had to close her eyes. The light burned through her and the world turned dark. She sat down heavily on the verandah step and wrapped her bony elbows around her knees. She was overwhelmed by the pointlessness of everything. There was no point in games. She couldn't remember the last time she got exactly what she would have wished from anything. She wanted to hide in the painting of the Orchard, listening for the footsteps of the hidden deer. She wanted the springtime and Acantia's light smile, to hear the whisper of the paintbrush against the masonite. She couldn't remember the last time she had heard it.

Goats won't live in houses but they will eat them on occasion, Siegfried observed in his goat diary.

Count Ugolini out of the blue persuaded Acantia to get Ursula a horse. 'Riding a horse is very good for a girl her age,' he said. And he knew just the horse. Ursula had saved a hundred dollars from two years of picking ixodia, a wildflower they all picked over summer. One day it vanished from her secret hiding place, and the next day Count Ugolini arrived with a horse float and a fine-limbed sorrel yearling crashed and clattered off the ramp and bolted into the bush. Ursula had seen her for all of twenty seconds and was beside herself with terror that this wasn't what it seemed.

'Six hundred dollars! Pure Arab!' Acantia said, hugging Ursula. 'You can owe me five hundred. You can pay me when you're a grown-up.'

Ursula pursued Ember for three days until the horse gave up, hungry and thirsty. Ember was everything Ursula's dreams had conjured and more. For one thing Ursula had not imagined that she would be so vicious, so unpredictable. It didn't matter. Ursula left the world of her siblings for a finer one, at times inconvenienced by pain and damage inflicted by her companion. By the time Ember was eighteen months old, Ursula had slipped up onto her back and learned to ride by clinging there wherever Ember went. She tried to limit the horse's movements by placing a pile of lucerne hay in the direction she wanted Ember to choose. Inevitably, Acantia caught her. The punishment in those golden months was light. Acantia was secretly impressed. She absolutely refused a saddle, but allowed a bridle.

Ember was never broken in. Ursula only ever got half mastery, even with a bridle. She taught the horse tricks and on a good day could do everything a normal riding twelve year old would do—jumping, bending, barrel racing, elementary dressage. On a great day she could do what few kids would consider with her bareback stunt riding. On a bad day she could do a fair demonstration of riding a buck-jumper, or cling on wherever Ember decided to bolt.

Siegfried loved goats. He loved them from their little beards to their neat cloven hooves, from the tips of their feathered tails to the points of their curled horns. He loved them for butting things and for the sly sideways looks they gave when they reared high and tucked their chins in the seconds before their horns connected. They seemed to him sophisticated and clever. He cackled at their jokes and his brothers and sisters laughed at him.

Siegfried became Siegfried Siegenbalg, or Ziggy Goatskin, when he was about seven. He took over the care of the goats and developed a herding instinct of a feral kind. Under his tutelage the goats became feistier. He roamed the goats' paddock headbutting them. He developed two little red marks on his forehead where Mars and Pluto's horn ridges made contact. The goats began interpreting the erect stance of humans as the preliminary to a play fight and would meet anyone game to walk past their wood pile on their hind legs, forelegs tucked and chins in, ready for the snaking downward plunge to crashing head contact. Ziggy began headbutting everything.

The night of the solstice, Acantia and Ursula are in the goats' shed with a torch. Acantia looks down on the mother and baby. India, who is Venus's great-granddaughter, grumbles lovingly at the tiny white kid as it shakes itself clumsily at her side. Life is running through it like the water of a thaw-flushed river. It tries to express its feelings in an athletic twist but succeeds only in shaking itself off balance.

India looks at Acantia, her eyes both soft and hard as amber, but doesn't move when Acantia touches the baby's silk hair with her fingertips. Ursula watches dreamily as her mother's fingertips brush its side, over its ribs, gently stroking the length of its faun back.

'Its name is . . . Anatta.' She stretches her arms to the night sky and Ursula looks up too. 'Anatta will be *free*, one day. She'll escape!'

They walk back to the house together.

Acantia says quietly, staring up at the stars.

'Life is a wonderful thing.'

A fox calls into the stillness. It is the sound of desire, cold and clear, rushing between the stars and the earth and then hanging there like a stain in the heart and sky after the sound has dissipated.

They all hated the billy Augustine. Whenever anyone went near him, he salivated and slapped his tongue in and out, snorted, stamped and moaned. Too close, his smell was overwhelming. He tried his hardest to piss on people. His penis was nearly always extended. The end of it looked as though it was tied in a knot and when he was bored he licked it or sprayed his forelegs. He was always bored, desperate and chained up. He had a pathetic, hormonally-deranged look in his eye. He was a slobbering bundle of pent-up semen and saliva.

After a while Siegfried could not stand it any longer. He took Augustine in the middle of the night up the hill, into the bush and over the back fence. There he released the putrid collar and shooed the billy off to go and find the wild goats beyond Acantia's boundary.

Augustine, exiled to freedom, stood at the boundary fence wailing all night.

The next day Acantia sent them all out on a search party and the goat found them easily.

The following year Augustine was the centre of a minor miracle. It even got into the papers.

When the two kids, Martyr and Satyr, were only three weeks old, their mother died of mastitis and joined the other cows, chooks and goats in the mass grave. Siegfried started to feed them with a bottle and they soon developed the scours. Just when it seemed as though the young goats would die, Augustine befriended them. One day, standing in his charmed stench circle, he nudged the babies along his body until their noses were buried in his flanks either side of his heavy bag of testicles. He stood there with his eyes closed, his legs apart and his tongue out. Martyr and Satyr appeared to be drinking, bumping his flanks so hard that the testicles swung, knocking their tiny chests. At first no one could believe this and no one wanted to go up to him and feel up there to see what was going on. Acantia sent Ursula to check. Augustine had little teats high up the sides of his scrotum and was making milk.

Siegfried squeezed his own nipples thoughtfully.

Goats are capable of anything if they put their minds to it, Siegfried wrote in his goat diary, and inserted the news clipping.

FATHER SUCKLES TWINS: GOAT MIRACLE

Yesterday at Whispers Farm, situated a mile past Deviation Road in our own Witlers Gully, our Photographer Denny Buzzard snapped this world wonder.

Nine-year-old Siegfried Houdini here proudly shows us his pet billygoat Augustine, suckling twins.

Professor Alex Daly of the Zoology Department of Toggenberg University said to our reporter today, 'Goats are pretty strange. As mammals they are the stranger in our midst.

'Some of them actually suckle from themselves, male and female.

'I can't say I'm the least bit surprised. They are capable of anything.

'Billygoat milk is extremely rare. I personally have never had the privilege of witnessing this phenomenon until today.'

Under the goats' guidance, Ziggy became resourceful, brave and creative. Ruth was a pure white goat. She had soft short hair, straight ears and fine legs. Her eyes were large and of a pale straw yellow. You could only tell what she was thinking if you watched her nose and ears. As soon as you looked at her eyes you couldn't be sure. She was going to be eaten for Christmas.

'Lilo,' Ziggy whispered, 'I am going to build you a flying car, a helicopter house. It will be for you and Ruth and no one else.'

Lilo didn't believe he could at first, but Ziggy described its mechanics in such detail and with such assurance that she could visualise it.

Lilo dreamed of Ziggy's car. It was long and black, and had both wheels and wings. She could see herself scooting up the driveway. The vessel was designed so that she sat in the front and Ruth stood behind her. Ziggy would build it, for he was the Great Inventor. Ziggy was one of the gods.

'Ziggy Goatskin Ziggy Goatskin / Achtung, Fertig, Dustbin,' Lilo chanted, willing the car to be born.

They ate Ruth for Christmas.

Ziggy spent more and more time with the goats and less time inside the house. He spoke goat fluently and the goats, usually incapable of any collective thought or action, united against anyone Ziggy disliked.

Ziggy started sleeping in the goats' shed. But one by one the rebellious goats were shot, eaten, sold or given away.

THE CASTLE

They all knew that they were in that castle. Its turrets gleam wet in the lurid air. A thick streak of Prussian blue lies alongside a scar in cadmium yellow on the aged stone parapet linking the castle to the bridge. The bridge is made for horsemen and is high above a darkened ravine. It has arches like those of a Roman aqueduct. The pillars of the arches extend out of sight into the darkness below. This was the favourite of most of the children as teenagers.

They were there.

The scene is set in the first torrent of a storm breaking. Cadmium lightning straight from the tube scores the sky, bursting from a magenta-hearted cloud. The courtyards are open to the sky, bare and deserted. The bridge is impassable and is the only way out.

This painting was many things for them. It was the gateway, the prison, the place of seclusion, safety, danger, depending on the game it had to illustrate. It was the moment of entrance into the medieval world. Ursula had been in other worlds. She too had brushed through the snow-covered spruces to the other side. She had been drawn, following the golden apples to the land where the shadows lie. The painting was the mirror through which she too could re-enter.

It had a grand story to it.

It was in Germany, long, long ago.

The Houdinis had stopped by a field of rye on the way to the castle. They climbed through the electric fence to have a picnic in the heavy sunlight of unpredictable late autumn weather. They had beautiful grey-brown stoneware plates back then, speckled like curlew eggs. They had left the car door leaning against the fence and Gotthilf got a shock when he reached out to get into the car. They all laughed but he felt a bit sick.

When they arrived at the mountain Acantia decided to stay in the car and the rest of them climbed the mountain to the castle with Pa. Ursula walked across that bridge as Pa told a story about the captured prince who was to be executed.

Asked if he had any last wishes, he said, 'Yes indeed. I would like to bid farewell to my horse.'

When they brought him his horse (which, as a precaution, was neither saddled nor bridled), he kissed it and vaulted onto its back. His horse was so loyal that when the bridge was barred by soldiers it leapt without hesitation over the parapet, bearing its rider to freedom. Ursula looked over the parapet. She wasn't convinced by the last part but Pa insisted that they fell into the waters of the moat which used to be there.

While they were in the castle the storm which had been brewing broke violently directly above. The Houdinis and a few other foolhardy tourists had no choice but to wait inside the thick cold walls until it was over. The children shivered, complained, got cold, got hungry. The water ran down the lichen-covered walls.

Acantia, far below, painted furiously. In the height of the violence the car was struck by lightning. She painted on, feverishly, praying that they would be delayed in the castle and that the car would have lost the electrical charge by the time they arrived at the foot of the mountain. The water poured out of the sky and she painted on. They huddled high above her under the darkening turrets. By the time they made it down they were wet and tired and cross. The car was washed safe and the painting was finished.

It is a castle in a storm, as seen from somewhere above the head of the access bridge.

Soya beans and unhappiness went together like winter mornings and ice puddles, but that hadn't always been the case. Ursula and Gotthilf and Beate remembered when the Houdinis had been happy and well fed and willpower had had nothing to do with it. They wondered what secret, silent bomb had blown them up when they weren't paying attention. Beate thought Pa had tried to leave Acantia once, had had an affair in Germany, and had stayed with Acantia *for the sake of the kids*.

It took the fight out of Ursula. They were all at fault. Her limbs went numb and her mind cloudy. To think that Pa might have said such a thing.

The theory wasn't popular at first. Most of them didn't want him to be implicated. He was their solace. Most of them didn't want to be implicated either. However, over the years Ursula embellished the concept so effectively that this idea became an accepted fact. Among the terrible betrayals of Acantia's life, her husband had stopped loving her and had tried to leave her.

If he was there for the sake of the kids, who was there for the sake of Acantia?

Although Ursula occasionally remembered they had made up the explanation, she knew that something had happened and that soya beans marked the spot like texta on a calendar.

When they came back from Germany, they ate soya beans for six months. Pa ate everything but wasn't keen on soya beans.

Acantia said that times were hard.

Acantia made soya bean salad (cooked soya beans, onions, lemon, oil and salt) as their first meal in Australia. Pa said nothing. He didn't even burp. Soya bean porridge was soya beans cooked and vitamised with some milk. Soya bean coffee was soya beans roasted and ground. They ate lecithin instead of honey on soya bean loaf. Soya bean stew was soya beans cooked for a long time. Pa made no sound and ate them up.

So did they.

By the end of six months, during which they left the great world and found Whispers, Ursula was so sick of soya beans that she thought she might die. Then, one day, Acantia said that the hard times were over and various foods reappeared. However, food was the only thing that improved. Soon most of them forgot what life had been like before.

No one stole soya beans.

An army fights on its belly. The children trained in secret as guerrillas and raiders. An act of considerable bravery was the theft of something obvious and needed for that night's dinner. A portion, or even the entirety, of a packet of shredded bacon, for example. Not a common item in the fridge. Such major crime was rare. However, under the impact of sustained minor pilfering everything turgid sagged gradually and everything richly coloured slowly paled as it was leached away and topped up with water. Dark grape juice became see-through, taut sacks of wheat and flour acquired wrinkles and inched away. Eggs disappeared warm.

In season, lollies saved up for birthdays or Christmas were hunted down like rare game. By the time they had to track down the phone key they were all skilled guessers of Acantia's thinking. They had no one to call, but Arno had to know where the key was, so they would all find it for him. Acantia succeeded in hiding very few items of food or entertainment from the children. The only things left to her were her secret past and her unpredictability.

Acantia placed hairs from her own head over jam jars, sealing the fridge door, around the cheese. The children eased the fridge door open, removed and then carefully replaced the black strands after watering the jam, shaving the cheese. They were banned from opening the fridge, so it had to be done with silent easing of pressure with the fingertips onto the doorseal, making it open with a sigh not a smacking kiss. The door seal wore out quickly.

Acantia tried cooking one less dinner than she had children, to flush out the prematurely satiated. But the terror of going without anything made them all rush up, jostling and noisy, when called. She made the last go without anyway. And then a bad tempered, importunate crowd of seething bodies pressured around her whenever she called them, even if softly.

The cook in her withered and died. It was war. They stole everything and, as they got older and bigger and more desperate, they were not surreptitious about it.

When a new flour sack had had its bottom corner cut off to replenish some private store, Acantia lined them up from Beate to Arno.

'Own up, whoever did this, or by golly I'll strap the lot of you!'

They had long grown out of accusing each other and stood in silent solidarity. She swung the reins around Beate's obediently extended wrists and went down the line. When she got to Helmut she whacked him with all her might, for she was sure that he had done it. When she got to Arno she swung extra light, for Arno was her angel. She had only reached Siegfried when Arno started giggling, snickering uncontrollably, nervously, behind his hand. As they left, nursing their arms, Arno was still giggling. He had got away with it. Taking a beating ensemble for so daring and stupid a raid was worth it. They all loved Arno's happiness. They all did anything for Arno.

Arno learned to read and write and play chess and do long multiplication without anyone teaching him. He collected hair, his own and that of his siblings. He spun and plaited from it a fine rope, which, by the time he was seven, was more than a mile long and had to be stored in a bucket. He was inconsolable when he found that moths had eaten the first few furlongs from the bottom of the bucket, and everyone cut their hair and gave it to him to cheer him up.

Ursula was something of a perfectionist and was proud of the length of time she was able to go without washing either herself or her trousers. She rode bareback summer and winter and washing her trousers removed the thick layer of horsehair embedded in them and made her feel the cold. In summer her legs were always two-tone. The insides were clean from horse sweat.

Ember stares with a familiar, capricious, perhaps-I-hate-you-today look and will not let herself be caught. Ursula, as always, persists until she can grab some mane and vault on. It is a move that impresses, both her and any real or imaginary onlookers. It has style. Ursula rides bareback, twisting and prehensile as a monkey. Over the flying hooves she crouches, her face to the wind, her eyes streaming tears, grinning, somehow floating in a bed of violent muscles, sweat and satin hair. She rides with whispers to Ember from her thighs, calves and heels, tiny coded signs which Ember can choose to ignore but knows well enough. She rides with no bridle, pretending that she is in control but really just sticking like a baby chimp regardless of the mean surprises the horse springs on her. This is Ember's opportunity and she exploits it with passion and invention.

Ursula prided herself on her trick riding, on the vaults, falls and daring pick-ups she could sometimes do, if Ember would cooperate. But she could never ride standing up, surfing a gallop. Ember wouldn't permit it.

Ursula was in love with Ember's beauty. She spent hours simply staring, touching grooming, and later covering up any bruises on her arms that were horse-inflicted. Sometimes the horse was loving, her huge black eye soft and sweet, blowing gently through her perfect nostrils onto Ursula's cheek. Sometimes she did everything Ursula asked, leaping and quivering.

Ember was, except in springtime, always too thin. For a while she was allowed to eat a quarter of what the cow got, since the cow had four stomachs.

Ursula twined her legs and arms around Ember's hot copper body when the horse was grazing, making sure she didn't take too much grazing time with riding. She read books, stretched like Mowgli along the horse's back, elbows propped against the broad rump. She sneaked extras in hay and bran and cooking oats to secret rendezvous points with her impatient beast. Ember became thinner and increasingly snarky.

Then Acantia noticed her staring ribs and angry eyes (the horse's, that is).

'That horse will have to be sold. You have obviously lost interest and cannot be trusted to look after it properly.'

Ember's feed bill was added to Ursula's account to pay back when she was a grown-up, and Ursula began to resent every mouthful the cow ate.

Ursula planned the great escape into the outback. She would live the life of a bushranger, simple and free (hunted intermittently by Acantia and her Troopers).

But in her heart she knew that if she really escaped there would not be room for two. She would be leaving Ember behind.

Ursula sat beside Gotthilf helping him milk the cow. He told her a joke about a woman's letterbox and a postman and a letter. He was angry when she didn't get it and told her what rape really was. Ursula was sceptical. She needed more than a delinquent's word for that. Gotthilf screamed at her suddenly that she was mentally retarded and didn't know anything. He was crying with rage. His tears dropped into the milk and for a moment made a bluish space before they disappeared.

They bundled into the kombi, stacked it up with blankets and headed off for the Murray. Acantia checked out properties along the way, pointed out Count Ugolini's vineyards and said odd and gentle things now and then, like, '*We'll* be OK'. Ursula wondered if those who would not be OK included the other kids and her father at home. Acantia also bought unusually unhealthy food when off alone with them. Pies and pasties and beer-battered fish. Sometimes there were leftover chips which they fed to the seagulls, happy with the wonderment of stomachs so full that chips could be given away. Acantia enjoyed it and enjoyed the children enjoying it. It was obligatory to be happy.

They were all very happy to get home. The children bounced on the bench seats, hooted and screeched as they crept along the winding track and the encroaching bush swallowed the kombi:

We are home
we are home
we are himmy home
we are home.

The kids who stayed home had it better. As soon as Acantia left, Pa howled joyously and raced off to the shops and bought olive oil, margarine, bread, salami, jam, lemons and anything else suitable for the occasion, raced home again and threw together massive piles of food: hacked-up chunks of bread and salami and, '*Simbalabim!*' conjured huge salads. They gathered around and helped themselves, oil dripping off their happy chins. He grinned and served and chewed with his mouth open, while they did their best to compete and stuff the lovely lighthearted day into their mouths as fast and as securely as they possibly could.

Then they would wander outside into the sun and bask or gather around a huge fire and doze, thigh to thigh, stinking and steaming into the humid air, while Pa tuned his viola in the auditorium and played dances.

They met their Uncle Lochie, Acantia's brother, once. He looked a little like Count Ugolini, for he was male and grown up, but otherwise resembled Acantia. He was seen to be a man of daring, dash and derring-do. He stayed for a day and influenced their thinking for three years. It was apple season. He went for a walk with the excited kids scampering at his heels. He leapt nimbly into Mr Vatzek's, stole three apples from the well-tended orchard and then leapt back over the barbed wire, swing! Just like that.

'Stolen fruit tastes sweeter,' he said, biting into a codlin larva.

Stolen fruit tastes sweeter, they whispered to each other at any moment that called for bravery or laughter. Stolen fruit tastes sweeter.

Uncle Lochie was engraved on their hearts in the space of six syllables.

A few years later a letter came from Uncle Lochie saying he would arrive on the first of April. Just like him. He was such a wag. Everyone was shot through with excitement. They woke up in the morning excited and went to bed exhausted from it and dreamed of Uncle Lochie. They raced around with fervour cleaning up the house. *Leave it Leave it*, the house sighed, *he can't possibly care and besides he won't really come*, but they ignored it and brushed its unruly hair. The great day came. They had all read the letter, they had all read the flight confirmation. Hugging the day to their leaping chests they piled into the car, no delays, quicksticks, and headed into Toggenberg town to the airport.

'Yip Yip Yip. Hey Hey Hey,' their hearts sang.

They waited in the arrivals hall, sitting perfectly still on the blue plastic seats. Uncle Lochie's plane landed and Beate started to laugh. She laughed so much she got embarrassed and started to cry. She cried so much she had to go to the toilet.

Uncle Lochie was not on it. Many people who were not Uncle Lochie came off, parted around them, and evaporated. They waited.

'Maybe he played a trick on us,' Gotthilf said hesitantly.

They started to laugh, a little wanly. It was very, very clever, you had to give him that. He really got them a good one.

'Would the Houdini family come to the Ansett information counter please. Would the Houdini family come to the information counter please.'

They looked at each other in wonder. Acantia and Pa led the way.

There on the information counter was a huge box and a letter. Uncle Lochie had been called to fix a burst oil platform in Kuwait and apologised for being unable to come in person. He wished them a happy Easter. His handwriting was a lot like Acantia's because they had been to the same school.

Inside the box was a dragon's treasure of Easter eggs, Easter rabbits, chocolates and glittering trains with Easter egg carriages. Wealth beyond compare. They were beside themselves. It was such an up and down trick, a disappointing, delicious trick.

A little note on top of the treasure said, *Stolen fruit*.

They went home laughing and shouting, expectant, sad and happy. At home they invited Easter in early and sat down to sort through a whole table load of riches.

Among the Easter eggs Gotthilf found a Toggenberg Centre Supermarket docket. Their eyes popped out of their heads as the truth slowly sank in. They pored over the letters, shrieking with laughter. They wondered over the secretive smile of the Ansett lady, the furtive smiles the other staff had given them. They laughed at the energy with which they had cleaned the house.

'April FOOOOOOOLS!' Acantia said, dancing, her face lovely with bright, overflowing laughter.

Pa did a little skip in the middle of the floor and they all sat around stuffing themselves with chocolate.

Goats eat whatever they like whether it's good for them or not, Ziggy wrote in his goat diary when Pieta ate the Easter egg wrappers.

When Acantia and Pa went on holiday to New Zealand, Ursula stayed to mind the place. They had a Saanen goat, called Teresa, with an odd chronic illness. Ursula watched her hobble with finicky steps past the window and acted without thought. She called the vet.

The vet explained the incurable disease, the suffering the goat had been in for the last six months and how long it would take her to die if nothing was done about it.

The blood beat in Ursula's head. A black horror opened up inside her ribcage and her voice fluttered out like a bat from a cave, telling him to put Teresa down.

She sat with the goat's head in her lap, watching the yellow eyes calm and fade as the vet eased a shockingly large amount of straw-coloured liquid into her jugular vein. Ursula was dizzy, flying without control.

The vet offered to help bury the body but Ursula refused.

She sat in the bracken, disbelieving even when the dirty white body went cold. It took her three hours to bury it. The hole in her chest was swallowing her up. A feeble, piping, self-righteous voice told her that she had done the right thing, but the gathering roar at the heart of the cave warned that for the rest of her life she would be alone in knowing it.

Ursula broke the news on the phone. Acantia didn't say much. When she got home, she asked to see the grave. Her face was serious. Acantia told Ursula that the vet's diagnosis was tragically ignorant and that she had returned home with the cure for Teresa from a goat expert in New Zealand. She said that Ursula had been too lazy to nurse the goat to health and had taken a disgusting way out.

Ursula was eleven, a criminal and a murderer. There was no consolation.

The vet bill was added to her account, now an impossible eight hundred and forty dollars to be paid to Acantia when she was grown up.

The next time Acantia went on holiday with Pa and the children, Ursula stayed home again, waving them all off amid jokes about not killing off any more goats. She roamed around happy, the self-sufficient princess buried in the forest. She wandered from animal to animal, taking more care of them than usual, because she and they were special when she was home alone.

Fundevogel the kitten was quiet and miserable, staying in one spot most of the day. Ursula picked him up and he screamed. She felt him all over and, with her scalp crawling, touched a spongy mess filled with little rocks and shards where his firm cat pelvis should have been. He was panting, stretched out on her lap. She sat by the phone waiting for Acantia to call. When the call finally came Ursula gabbled hysterically about calling the vet. There was silence on the end of the line. Then Acantia said quite gently, 'What's the matter? Who is ill?'

Ursula's teeth chattered.

'Fundevogel! His pelvis is completely smashed! I have to call the vet!'

Acantia said calmly, 'Someone must have slammed the door on him. I thought there was something wrong with him before I left. You will have to put him down. It's the humane thing to do, and I know how seriously you take that. You are a courageous girl. Get a bucket and some rocks and make the water warm so it is more comfortable for him. Now stop working yourself up. You have killed things before.'

'I have to call the vet!'

'No. That you may not do.'

The phone clicked like a light switch.

Fundevogel lay in Ursula's lap in a daze. She laid him out on the floor, averting her eyes from his life-in-death form, while she prepared everything as Acantia had said.

He fought but she was stronger. He bit through her hand between the thumb and forefinger. Blood spread in the green bucket like purple smoke. When he was limp, Ursula held the kitten's mouth to her lips, but then breathed in slowly, tasting water. *If I bring him to life I will only have to kill him again*. She went up into the bush cuddling his body. Now she was truly a murderer and she was back in Acantia's world. She wandered down the hill, looking at the animals with hatred. She let the cow go hungry, her resolve strengthening with every bellow.

Ursula lay in the dark house alone through the long nights until everyone returned. Acantia hugged her tightly. She said Ursula was very brave and Ursula soaked up all the comfort she could get. Acantia brought the light and peace back with her and Ursula was able to sleep.

Never forsake me and I will never forsake you, the kitten told her in her dreams and she was comforted.

Pa didn't appear much in Ursula's diary—there was barely a mention of him. But Ursula was dismayed to find that she didn't appear in his. Not at all.

As she made his bed one morning she found a black leather notebook in his blankets. She was safe as long as she could hear him playing. She snuck off to the edge of the bush and sat down to read it out of sight.

It was written in German. Although she didn't know some of the words, she could follow the gist of it. It was full of comments on European culture, art, poems, quotes from whatever book Pa was reading, and snippets of music. She hummed them to see whether they were familiar. They were not. She skimmed the last two-thirds, looking for her name, looking for any of their names.

She shut the book and stared up at the stringybarks, feeling very lonely. The diary covered a period of about three months. Big things had happened in that three months. She had improved on the violin, and excelled in her lessons—these were things that seemed to matter a lot to Pa. She had murdered a goat and a kitten, and had stayed at Whispers alone for two whole weeks while he went with everyone else to New Zealand. She had turned twelve.

She felt flooded with anxiety. Nothing was really as it seemed.

The viola trilled and wailed to nobody across the paddocks.

Pa wasn't really on their side at all.

wolf notes

Helmut and Siegfried started Christmas jokes. The first were droll puns and bad word play, usually born over Christmas dinner. They were burpets and farticles—jokes of bad taste and minor wit. But Christmas jokes evolved into quirky gilt-edged criticism of the family's pain, an end-of-year concession to suffering, a surreptitious goading notice to Acantia that the children were vaguely aware that not all was well; and, in effect, an acceptance.

One Christmas dinner when everyone was in high spirits, the twins started a casual conversation about the names of prospective children.

'Whaddaya gunna name ya kids?' Siegfried said into the air, but everyone knew he was addressing Helmut.

'Oh, I like the name Victoria,' Helmut said, turning with an engaging and serious face to Siegfried.

'For myself,' Siegfried said, sucking thoughtfully on a drumstick, dropping the Aussie drawl, 'I think Timothy is a lovely name for a boy.'

Acantia looked at them brightly. Everyone else could tell something was up.

'You all have lovely names. When you have children we will all help!'

'Between us, we could have one of each. "Victooria! Teeeeee-mothy!"' Helmut experimented with a peremptory summons.

'Yep, I think Victoria and Timothy are the names for me,' Siegfried said.

'But they will get called Vic and Tim!' Acantia wailed in protest.

Beate told Ursula they were cruel. She was right but even she couldn't stop laughing.

'G'day Vic,' Ziggy would say.

'Howdy Tim.'

The others began calling either twin Victim and the joke was banned.

'Children. Keep your minds clean. Bad thoughts make bad people. If you desire evil that is what you will bring into the world. I desired *goodandgoodonly* and I brought you into the world. If I wanted you dead, Ursula, you would die. I would only have to point the bone, like the Aborigines. It's all in the mind.'

As they grew up and began to desire more than mental cleanliness, the demands on the house's resources increased dramatically. Helmut and Siegfried got hygiene late but when they did, the pressure on both houses was intense.

Acantia tried ridicule:

The vanity of teenage boys has no limits.

Acantia tried sabotage:

Teenage boys do not need underpants.

Acantia tried science:

Hot water gives you pimples.

Acantia tried prohibitions:

Thou shalt not use soap.

But in the end the simplest methods work best.

When the shower broke down she refused to get it repaired. This lasted two years.

But the wiles and cunning of the young are infinite.

It started with the great nudist rebellion, pioneered by Lilo. Having broken the nude barrier in the privacy of their bedrooms, Lilo, Siegfried, Helmut and Arno were fledglings ready for first flight. One day, when Acantia and Pa weren't home, Lilo's glimmering white body walked outside into the sunlight and tried to act casual, to go about its ordinary business. The naked boys emerged almost immediately from their hiding places and the fledglings stretched their new wings in solemn joy. After that whenever Acantia and Pa were out the clothes fell off and they scampered outside in all their ribby adolescent beauty, pale white skin radiant in the sunlight. They played Gotthilf's KISS tape in the auditorium.

They ran about the yard shrieking, ran up the hill, strolled in a leisurely way, took the air, and sprinted for cover, the excited dog leaping and snapping dangerously close, when they heard the car labouring up the other side of the hill. They soon extended these stolen pleasures to the group scrub-up under the garden hose.

Then one day Lilo walked out in front of the kitchen window and calmly showered under the jetting hose in front of Acantia and Pa. Before they could react the boys joined her, and their four youngest children twirled their new pubic hair, glistening skin and shining bellies in a silent and aggressive dance in front of them. They passed the soap around and made eye contact only with each other. It lasted a few frozen minutes and then they scattered, shrieking and whooping with victory and giddy freedom.

They didn't put their clothes on again that summer. For a while Acantia was at a loss and then she started painting them.

They speculated over what might have happened to Acantia. She was the rebel, the beautiful young woman who refused to be a debutante and didn't shave her legs. Acantia who toured around Australia on a motorbike in the fifties, accompanied only by her dog. Floosie was a border-collie cross with natural bikie glasses. In an old (and later scorched) photograph Acantia is shooting her mysterious, riveting smile at a camera which also takes in her long thigh and tanned leg. She sits at ease on the machine, looks at once utterly feminine and warriorlike. This was the Acantia who flashed a knife in the moonlight at the men trying to force their way into her isolated tent. Acantia who hitched alone and broke across Europe, who taught kids in London slums, who beat up a truckie who tried to tongue-kiss her. It was all suggested in those black and white photos of a wild, dark girl, so stunning that Beate always said, 'No wonder Pa fell in love with her!' and sighed.

On the other hand they had the Acantia they knew.

Acantia now and then developed a manic desire for cleanliness. But even washing the dishes clean was impossible, for she didn't believe in any kind of cleaning agent. The house muttered, *Don't bother it can make no difference*, and the children listened and stashed the dirty saucepans under the plum tree. Many years of no soap and rancid tea towels had left everything with a receding useable centre and a periphery of caked, greasy, cooked-on grime. Glasses left prints on their fingers. The windows were almost opaque, filmy and dim. Only at night could they see clearly through the glass, and that was when they watched the Tarsinis the way other people watched television.

Acantia began to make her own soap from goat fat. Old honey vats were filled with the fresh lard from the latest slaughter, filling the kitchen with the reek of billygoat and murder.

Varnishing the floor was the exception. It was a big job and Acantia and Ursula were a team. Ursula worked in wordless harmony with Acantia, transforming the house with one cataclysmic effort into something different. It was magical. None of this effort was pointless. It had a path and a pattern and the sequence led sensibly and predictably to the glory of the new-polished floor and an echo of the happiness of their first arrival at Whispers. Side by side, stamina and attention to detail rewarded, they smiled tiredly at each other at the end of the days. Covered in the same dust, smiling the same smile.

But the house wore Acantia out. After Ursula left home she decided that the floorboards could not sustain any more sanding and oiled the floor with some of the excess goat fat instead. From then on it joined the ranks of the utterly uncleanable. Impregnated with a sticky, viscous suet and tramped over by countless work boots carrying slush and dust and slush again, it could do nothing except collect, fester and wait for the fire.

The first crosshatched paintings had something elusive and wonderful.

Acantia said that the downwards brushstroke was the descent of divine inspiration (or the supplication of life yearning for and receiving inspiration), and the horizontals were the waiting world. It was Water and Earth. She said the secret of the universe, material and spiritual, was revealed in her brushstroke.

A sky is suspended refractive, having the striated distortions of moving water. Liquid and structured, somehow not possible but resonant. The gossamer skies suggested something beyond their infinite colours but you could never say what. Acantia's skies reflected the world below as seen in a frozen pool. It was an icy, forbidding sky that loomed so glorious over the earth.

The world occasionally imitated her paintings. The day of the first bushfire the clouds reflected the flames in strangely geometric fragmentation.

When Ursula stared at Acantia's great paintings, she wanted to fix the world for her mother. She went into frenzies, cleaning and polishing the centre of the kitchen floor when Acantia was out. To see her come home and her face lighten as she walked in was addictive. For a while Ursula believed she held the family together with these small polished pools. She developed a responsibility complex and the house hated her.

When things went crazy the house sneered at her. The expanses of filthy floor stared smugly up at her. *You could have prevented it somehow.*

Ursula experimented with body language. She pouted and flounced. She sneered, shrugged, retorted.

Little Bear found himself in most unwholesome circumstances. Enslaved, yes, but worse was to come. Those around him plotted for his very life. Little Bear was going to have to find where they had hidden Fireflame and hope he could outwit them. Fireflame was fast enough, he was sure, to carry him to freedom, but he had to get out of range of their weaponry. And what if they had cut her hamstrings, crippling her forever?

Ursula planned the great escape. She escaped secretly several times but nobody noticed, which made her feel as if she had failed even before she returned home. In fact she would return home to see if they had noticed and invariably find that they had not.

Her planning was impeccable. She escaped through Mr Vatzek's place, placing a white wooden beam on the barbed wire fence so that Ember could jump it in the dark, then removing it to a hiding place in the long grass on Mr Vatzek's side. Acantia had instilled in the children a great fear of Mr Vatzek. He chased them once when they crossed the border (it was before they had built the barbed wire perimeter fence), shouting, 'No Gots! No Gots!' and waving his stick. The stick seemed to turn into a snake, writhing and hissing, and even the goats were spooked. Mr Vatzek was seldom seen in person but inhabited their nightmares. Sometimes they saw him at dusk, hobbling like an old bent woman along the perimeter dividing their two worlds. Mr Vatzek's animals all had bits missing. His chooks were one-legged. His cows had their tails chopped off. His sheep had no ears. He had a donkey with its face all awry.

Ursula walked Ember down to Mr Vatzek's lake, tied her to a tree on a long line and lay down under the tall gumtrees, cushioned from all noise other than Ember's comforting sigh and heavy shuffle and the soft, secret conversations of birds and trees and wind. No one would even imagine that she would go this way. She camped out, shuddering with fear and something else under the beautiful darkness of the trees, the spangled sky glittering through their ragged black feathers. She could not sleep. She stared into the glimmering dark, listening, breathing. All was still. She tried to imagine that she was miles away, in Germany. But the black bowl of the sky above her looked too stale and homely. The stars were the tiny escape holes, letting in fragments of light from the real world. If she could get up there and squeeze her body through one of them, she would emerge into the light above like a cat from a drainpipe. She was like a kitten in a cardboard box, staring at the needle holes punched in it to let in air. A fox cried out from the hill above. *Wa-aah, wa-aah,* a ghostly voice hanging, eerie, like the stars themselves. She was filled with longing. The cry could carry her out like a thermal under her wings, raising her to the stars. She tried to focus on the glacial cries but her head was still trapped in the house. Images of the sleeping Houdinis floated up like dank steam into the night air and she started to cry.

Arno sleeps with his cheeks dirty in the dark, dirty with old tears no one understands. Helmut talks and burbles, as he always does when he sleeps. She looks at Siegfried, curled to the wall, his bedclothes stinking. She mentally flips him over, swinging his arm wide at a mosquito, leaving him with his face lit, dreaming, in a shaft of moonlight. The shadows under his eyes look like pools of blue ink. Lilo is asleep under her bed, cuddling a cat and six kittens. Gotthilf is lying on his tummy, naked in the moonlight as always, his buttocks gleaming and his head under the pillow. Beate in Beate's house is harder to see. Maybe she sleeps like a princess or a corpse—on her back, feet together, with her long golden hair splayed on the white pillow. Ursula has never crept in to stare at Beate sleeping and decides that she will, soon. The Houdinis rumble and rattle in concert, a warm sound percolating like a fart through the blankets and out through the room. Ursula imagines herself as the Tomten, singing a special song that only children understand. Looking in, being the Tomten, makes everything look sweeter.

She got tired of playing with their forms and looked up. Patches of stars glittered onto her face. How beautiful she must look in this light: pale face, gold-silvered hair, dark shining eyes. She would keep her mouth shut and soulful—*so*—to prevent its great width from being evident. She wouldn't grin and break the smooth planes. She jumped up and went down to the lake to stare at herself, but her face fell into deep shadow as she stared down at the water. Her hair, falling around her face, looked beautiful enough. She could just make out two star-like glimmers that had to be her eyes, looking back. The lake stared back at her like a huge, mysterious eye. The trees formed a pitch dark rim, thick lashes, and then the centre, still as still, caught each star. The Milky Way was spread in a shining convex band from corner to corner of the eye, giving it an almost completed luminosity, a strange, almost seeing, almost photographic quality. She stared at the water for a while and then sat down at the edge. Some tiny spot inside her glittered on. You reach an age, she thought sagely, when knowing what really is becomes impossible. You reach an age when you cannot know whether it is you or her. She suddenly felt very lonely. She looked down at her hands and imagined Burt's huge thick-skinned palm between them. Burt's blue-eye wink was such a long time ago. Her chest tightened.

Back at her hiding spot she lay down, still too alert to sleep. She stripped naked. She imagined his rough hands reaching out for her belly. She showed him everything there was to know, the catalogue of what a body transformed by escape and moonlight has to offer.

Ursula woke at dawn feeling ashamed, hating her body. She strapped her breasts down again with the strip of linen torn from the edge of her sheet. She went down to the lake, now streaked pink and grey and silver. She took a long stick and pierced the colours, thrusting the stick smoothly deep into the eye. The pink and grey shuddered and the reflective surface dissolved and she stared down into the clear, deep water. The stick went down down down, twisted. Where it met the water it bent suddenly and from then on went crooked. Her chest constricted and she went home slowly, taking no precautions. Mr Vatzek neither saw nor chased her. Ursula wished he had. She walked into the kitchen, her hair full of pine needles. Nobody noticed. She watched as, seemingly in slow motion, Acantia leaped like a giant and with a superhuman roar, tossed the table onto the floor and a saucepan, nine bowls of porridge, chairs and children scattered around the room. Porridge spattered the walls.

Acantia so liked to hear about the activities of delinquents that Ursula invented an encounter to please her. She pretended someone had stolen her bus fare by knocking her down. Acantia loved it and even told Count Ugolini. Ursula felt slightly guilty but Acantia's pleasure was satisfaction enough to soothe her qualms.

When a man at the bus stop showed Ursula his erect penis, lovingly, like a kangaroo giving birth, she didn't tell. She was afraid but also drawn: his solicitude for himself fascinated her. She was most afraid that Acantia would see through her and guess that she had been fascinated. Acantia always said that Ursula was the lascivious one and would have to watch her passions. From the age of nine Ursula watched them very closely, waiting to see what she meant. Sure enough, Acantia was right.

'My only regret is that I didn't knock the deceit out of you,' Ursula murmurs up close to the window glass. She watches Ursula Tarsini with hatred and disgust. There she is, sulking in the dirty glass. No doubt she also has to watch her passions, little lascivious liar. She has a surreptitious, sneaky face. Wide, full lips and prominent teeth. Green eyes. She has cropped lank hair and also wishes she was a boy. She looks like a boy. Like Huckleberry Finn, maybe. Tough and wiry. That is just one of her lies. Her breasts too are strapped flat with a piece of torn sheet.

Her face is rubbery and can contort into any number of expressions. That is another of her lies. Her face.

Ursula puts her lips up against the greasy window and crosses her eyes at Ursula Tarsini. Then she whispers, watching the lips form the words back at her, 'Liar, Liar, Pants-on-Fire.'

Ursula invented comforting when she was thirteen. She told no one because she wasn't one hundred per cent sure that comforting was OK. At first she tried not to think about it too much. She told herself that it could not possibly be as bad as tampons and she told herself that her ability to invent it showed genius and resourcefulness, both of which she was supposed to be developing. She could not sleep without it so it could not be too terrible. She curled her body around her own arm and, like a wild child, buried her fingers between her legs and rubbed herself to sleep with quick, licking, tender movements. When she did think about it she was pretty sure that Acantia would not approve of comforting, and to postpone indefinitely any real certainty on the matter she kept it to herself. She felt a little guilty. If comforting was in fact a brilliant new discovery, she was denying her brothers and sisters the benefit of it by her silence. She was relieved when one day she sprung Gotthilf comforting himself and then she was annoyed. What if she hadn't invented it at all? What if there was already an edict in force as to its legality? She began to make discreet inquiries, a difficult, almost impossible mission without giving too much of her position away. Still she comforted herself every night, but she began to wonder if this was simply her passions at play and not her genius at all. Her milk was soured and she felt an almost uncontrollable desire to ask everyone she met.

'Is comforting oneself an OK thing to do?' she finally asked Acantia outright, knowing that this was cheating and that Acantia wouldn't know the full extent.

'Of course.'

'Physically comforting oneself?' she persisted, her heart beating. Would Acantia guess?

‘What do you mean?’

Ursula’s vision began to black over.

‘Stroking,’ she said very softly, weak with terror. Suddenly, involuntarily, her hand crept up and, monkey-like, she began to stroke her own hair, patting her head until it became that of a child. Acantia laughed, grinning at her brightly.

‘Of course, you silly little nong.’

It was cheating but she had obtained a kind of permission. She tried not to think about it after that.

The castle rests at the bottom, below the line of vision, embedded in a dreary town all facades of mist-drenched grey. Green lichen stains the earth and sky. The great mountain dwarfs the keep, paws wrapped about the buildings in careless possession. Everything is sinking into the dank blue-green soupy colours and yet they all hold out firmly. It stands defensive, assailed by ravenous mists. Everything is a warp or a weft, every stroke horizontal or vertical. A solid and fractured sky, frozen stresses. But like a mantle over the mountain lies a further image, for the mountain is also a lioness. She rests there, regal, hidden in the deep, damp mists from the African sun.

Only Ursula could see her.

This huge painting filled one wall of the old music room. It was very beautiful but, without the lioness, as pressured as the bottom of the sea, as cold as their house in winter.

They picked ixodia all over the district, Acantia teaching them the wisdom of the ages in an enraptured voice in the mornings, and falling silent by the afternoons. The hills around Toggenberg gradually changed from unmapped wildernesses inhabited by strangers to being a series of places, named and fossicked through, with treaties and agreements set up through knockings on strange doors and answerings by people, one in fluffy slippers, another with a bald head and very long fingernails, another who smelled strange, and one whose penis hung out of his pyjama fly. The people who inhabited the Toggenberg hills were invariably sleepy, but less and less strange, as they became signposts to the known paths through to ixodia patches and as they entered Acantia's conversation in the evenings. Gradually they acquired names and characters. Most were poets, philosophers, Marxists and eccentrics holed away in the bush where no one would find them. Vincent Buckley lived in a post-and-mud shack on stone blocks surrounded by sculptures, and although he originally agreed to let the Houdinis pick ixodia on his craggy place, he drove them off a week or so later with yells of dismay when they accidentally picked the rich harvest around what Acantia said was the grave of his nine-year-old daughter, the inspiration for all his poetry.

'Poor man,' she said contritely, shaking her head. 'He always wanted to equal Wordsworth, but grief makes you unbalanced, and it's impossible to equal Wordsworth in Australia. You can paint Australia but you can't write good poetry about it. I haven't even read his poetry, but I can tell there's no point.' She waved sympathetically but dismissively at the clay sculptures, the bottoms, breasts and open-mouthed eyeless faces of several different sizes of woman.

Patrick White was another confused recluse who had retreated to the stark, glorious scrub of the Toggenberg hills, but he never opened his door when they knocked, and Acantia wasn't one hundred per cent sure he was *the* Patrick White, the one all the fuss was about. His books weren't up to much, she said, as they picked his slopes clean to see whether this would provoke him out of his hut. She'd read much better. She didn't understand why the psychologist would say that the kids were missing out on contemporary culture. Most of contemporary culture was made up of unhappy men who couldn't write good books and who made sculptures that showed sick mentalities, and in any case who ran away from contemporary culture to live in the Toggenberg hills to try to reconnect with the spirit. As she said this she stood up, red faced from climbing through the dry bracken, scratches on her arms and cheeks in white and red weals from the low but rampant blackberry and gorse. She put her hand into the small of her back and sighed, looking around. Ursula was above her on the slope, looking out over the wild valley. Ixodia dusted the escarpments of the steep opposing hill, bleaching the undergrowth under the few sinewy stringybarks. The orange earth showed through in patches, shimmering in the heat. Below them, on the rim of a stark orange dam, built for no purpose at the end of a steep overgrown track in otherwise unbroken bushland, stood a tiny billygoat, staring up at them. Acantia squinted up at Ursula, looking tired and sad under the sweat and dust, then looked away.

'Pretty useless,' she said, so softly that only Ursula's preternatural hearing and attunement to her mother could have recorded it.

Acantia sat bunching ixodia flowers, her back to the light. It was a moonless night and she faced nothingness like the captain of a spaceship. The floor was white with the tiny petals, green with the broken discarded stalks. The house looked like the aftermath of a wedding or a funeral, unkempt with flowers either strewn as confetti or shredded in wild bereavement. Scattered and piled about were enough flowers for more than a thousand celebrations or losses. Acantia was silent, moving rapidly, the air filled with the sappy click of stalks being broken. She was sitting on the step leading from the verandah to the paddock. Ursula was sitting directly behind her on the step leading from the house to the verandah. Her fingers, like Acantia's, were caked with the sticky, scabby green residue, the sap of countless green stalks. Her hands were green, ingrained, palms streaked from pressing the heads of the flowers together into a cauliflower shape, tired from snapping the rubber band around them and stacking them against the walls, where they formed white knobbly inner walls of everlasting flowers all around the house.

Acantia became obsessed with ixodia for several years running but Ursula's fourteenth year was definitely the worst. She didn't need the money but said that she did so passionately and so often that it was unquestioned fact. She stockpiled tens of thousands of bunches, supplies for an endless funeral. They walked through muffling corridors of flowers, crunching petals underfoot. The house walls and the paintings disappeared behind the mounting knobbled walls built from the frail roundish white bricks. She hoarded the money made from selling some to florists, saving to buy land, land and more land, enough for several cemeteries.

Flower season lasted for three months over summer. The children got a lot of good fresh air.

Ursula stared at Acantia's back. They were moving in unison, like rowers pulling at their oars, reaching into the water, hauling, paddling the verandah out into the darkness. One of Acantia's shoulders was always higher than the other, raised and twisted inwards. Ursula had never noticed before. Without breaking rhythm, she carefully raised and twisted her own, ducking her head in slightly until her body fitted the pattern of her mother's. Something flowed around her form, knocking blindly, lurching within her sudden asymmetry. It was the body shape of unhappiness, the vessel for discomfort, annoyance, misery. Acantia was unhappy. Ursula straightened, losing rhythm entirely. When did that happen? When did Acantia become silently miserable? When did she last see Acantia straight and smooth? She couldn't remember and started to panic. She tried to picture her mother that morning. The shoulders were hunched, the eyes were tense, like those of a cornered cat.

Acantia sensed the broken rhythm behind her and turned her head, holding it as though her neck was braced. She stared at her daughter out of an eye, shadowed in the stark light of the hallway, invisible in a triangular black pool under her brow. Ursula wanted to cry out, *I didn't see anything, No, nothing at all.* But she also felt a jolt of excitement and power. She knew something about Acantia. Something had leaked out and Ursula was in the right place at the right time to catch it. What a thing to know.

Acantia looked wild and fierce but her face was wet.

Ursula bunched furiously. If bandaging the house with flowers would fix it, that is what she would do. She was exultant.

Acantia roamed the hills with her children denuding them of white as efficiently as a plague of locusts. It took three years to sell off that summer's stockpile. In the end Acantia had enough pieces of land in various forgotten corners of South Australia that the Houdinis had homes away from home for all the surprise holidays Acantia sprung on them.

At age fourteen, out of the blue, Ursula had sex.

She found herself one morning as dead as Fundevogel, with no plans, no passions. Nothing. She looked at the clear sky and hated it. She thought of her brothers and sisters and felt nothing. She looked down at herself. She ran a distant hand over her breasts, her legs, her belly. When she held herself at arm's length she knew she had power over the pitiful rag pinched between her thumb and forefinger. But the normal seeming morning, with its shrieks, wails and viola, was making her panic. Horror was welling up her spine again, and she became aware that she was tearing at her own chest, beating herself. She could not bear to be trapped in this . . . this filth.

He had said she was lovely.

In the early years, when the woodman pressed Beate's small body up against the rough bark of the biggest pine tree and forced his tongue into her throat, Acantia and Pa were there to hear her scream. They ran out and told the woodman with outraged voices that they would not be buying wood from him again, and Gotthilf got the job of woodchopping.

'Self-sufficiency. We don't need wood *delivered*!' Acantia said. Wood delivery was the most outdated and ridiculous thing. The children laughed gaily, except for Beate, who was shaking, vaguely waiting for something else to be done about it all.

That was the last time Pa and Acantia were in earshot.

'Count Ugolini has offered to have you stay with him on his yacht.' Acantia fussed at Gotthilf's collar. Her voice was hushed, even envious. Gotthilf was standing dressed in a long white shirt several sizes too big for him. He was fifteen and looked silly. Acantia would not have him going to Count Ugolini's in dirty clothes. The shirt somehow satisfied her idea of waterborne medieval aristocracy. She could see her boy sitting there silent, dressed in white, playing duets or playing chess with the Count.

Gotthilf knew better than to protest. He had his concert trousers on underneath. He was a little excited. He would be out, away, almost free, having adventures. He had never heard Ugolini say much and had expectations of silence and the sea. He imagined saying at the beginning, 'I am enraptured with embarkation,' and at the end, 'Thank you, Antonio, for all the immeasurable kindnesses you have shown me. I am truly honoured to have been your submariner,' and not really saying much in between.

'You are a good boy. Do exactly what Count Ugolini asks you to.'

Count Ugolini was carving the roast. The children stared at his hands, quiet and still, vague pools of nothing for eyes. The slices looked like Russian dolls, each one size smaller than the last but identical.

His hands were wrapped around the broken bone knife handle and were almost the same colour. The blade slid forward and each slice formed a lip, then a mouth, then a cresting wave sinking onto its fellows on the plate, bleeding softly. After three slices Ursula wrenched her eyes away and then she caught a glimpse of Gotthilf's face, blank as a rabbit's in headlights.

A grey mist lifted and her body curled like a salted leech.

Gotthilf too, too! was all she could think. She sizzled with a strange envy and disappointment. Was he beautiful too? She stared at Gotthilf's miserable, pinched face, and suddenly felt much older than him; and gross to the heart. Her thin older brother was not beautiful. He looked broken—*her* body had brought the wolf into the fold. She was dizzy with the horror of it. She perversely almost hated Gotthilf for it.

Ugolini would perhaps have kept Ursula close. But he left it too long. By the time he visited after the yacht trip, Ursula had developed a terror of him so powerful that she was physically sick with fear and had to stay far away from his voice, body and breath.

When he wasn't there, being the person she had been before was as simple as shaking off a bad dream. Her terror was not of him so much as of the actuality of it. She felt dizzy with confusion. It was all a dream, it had to be. She wouldn't meet his pleading, commanding eyes; she wouldn't come near and shake his hand.

It was easy be the person she had been before, and forget. She headed off with Ember all day and no one thought that strange. She remembered dimly how much she had worshipped the Count after he got Ember for her, but that couldn't touch her now, or taint Ember. She smiled, suddenly, face to the wind, thinking of the time Ember bit him. Would have left a big bruise.

She tried to stop thinking about the Count altogether. She shaved her head and cut deep grooves into her thighs with the point of a knife. She fought the shifting patterns and tides of her terrible body.

And then it all faded and she could barely remember it. The sight of the Count's car made her feel an unpleasant tingle, a presence of something she never allowed near. She never thought about her distant hellos and goodbyes. She felt nothing and had school, now, to get on with.

Ursula liked school. She craved attention and at school she got it. School was a world of library, laboratory and lavatory, peopled by children. Ursula wandered around in a self-contained, unresponsive bubble. The aggression of children, their sideways looks and their attacks, increased the faint air of satisfaction she gave off. Gotthilf flickered at the edge of her vision, ignoring her and anchoring her. She was impervious. She excelled. She scratched incessantly, making permanent scars on her arms.

She was almost silent but quite happy. She concentrated on all conversations she had heard and stored, inserting the witty retorts she had not made, charming herself with what had almost been a conversation, a joust, a victory. She noted fourteen-year-olds' obsessions, their attention to boys, clothes, music, and felt very pleased with herself. She marked Carolyn Treloar as the one to beat in maths. She decided she liked jeans with the pockets low on the buttocks, rounding them, not higher, missing the buttocks altogether. She blushed when the boys threw tampons at her, but it was only her body that blushed. She was pleased with herself for recognising, with no prior experience, that they were tampons, and secretly delighted that she had guessed it would be social disaster to reach down and pick one up.

And just when the novelty was wearing off, and she had begun to writhe at being tied to the slow ticking hands of the clock, the children would do something so remarkable, so worthy of study, that she was caught again.

The kids called her Ershel Who Dunny. She corrected their pronunciation until she realised it was deliberate. They made toilet flushing noises as she passed. They called her Scritch-Scratch and Leper, and made bell tinkles to mark her passage. She imagined their changed hearts when she rescued them from the inferno.

'What does your father produce on your farm?'

Ursula thought about it. She guessed that something airy and superior about music would be risible, as Gotthilf would say. Pa didn't farm. She suddenly saw this as a lack, a failing on his part.

She knew with sudden clarity that none of these farm children must ever be allowed to see the Houdinis' whisperweed-choked fields and the weed drowned orchard. She blushed. How shameful to let land go to waste!

'Apples,' she said. The Houdinis had never actually brought in a whole harvest from the orchard, let alone sold an apple. But they did have six acres of orchard, and usually picked the tree by the house clean. 'Red Delicious, Johnnies and Strawberry Rose.' She was impressed with herself suddenly for how much she knew about apple cultivation. 'We had *enormous* problems this year with codlin moth, and spot. Had to *spray*. But the coolroom is full, nevertheless, because the season was that good, whaddayano. We get teams of pickers in, but it's really hard work in picking season, even with the pickers. The pruning is no fun either, but the trees like it. I can just *feel* the sap rising, and feel them thanking me for cutting away the dead wood . . .'

Ursula was alone in the shelter shed. She thought back through the conversation like a master chef tasting a failed experiment. *Just a touch overdone.*

School was like a story in which she was the heroic outcast, and so was almost inexhaustibly entertaining. Home was more confused, unpredictable. Home was real life.

Night after night Ursula lay in bed trying to prevent corrosion and decay. Every image in her mind became carious, melted, bubbled away into nothing. She flicked through images rapidly, trying to hold onto an object which would remain full and pure. But everything became disgusting. Everything beautiful was destroyed.

Sooner or later she would focus on her own feet, there in a V under the blankets. They emerged in her mind pearlescent, glowing pink. Then just as she was beginning to breathe easily and dive towards sleep, a tiny bubbling hole appeared at the base of the big toe. Her feet corroded and silently sizzled away to a flat irregular mass at the end of her legs. She focused on her legs, but they too burst in a fistulous mess and vanished away to almost nothing. As her body and her heart boiled away and died she stiffened with a frozen panic. She was left with the horrid sentient head fixed staring into the darkness, waiting hours through the night for the return of her body. She was powerless to bring it back. Usually she awoke next morning freed of the bad mood. She soon learned not to focus on things precious to her. The horse, the cat were off limits. But her body was fair game. By the time she was sixteen she enjoyed the uncontrollable mental destruction of her body and the panic peace it brought her.

KING INGOL AND THE WHIRLWIND

The evil King Ingol loved the flesh of boys and girls, although few knew this. He visited the castles of his neighbours and minions and was lavish in gifts, generous to a fault, and all loved him, except for the visionary princess Ariane, who had seen the way he looked at her brother, had seen the evil lust with which he pursued the boy. Elaan, her beloved brother, noticed nothing, and accepted the gift of the finest horse in Ingol's stable with youthful delight and gratitude. And Elaan would not heed her warnings, sure that his sister was jealous of the King's favour.

Time passed and Ariane watched in distress as the King earned the trust and confidence of her parents, and the friendship of Elaan. She was not sure what she feared, for she was a pure innocent, but she sensed the sensual, corrupt poison of the King's touch, and had seen children turn from bright youth to grey despair overnight in the village and was sure that the King was somehow responsible. Ariane alone could see that all greyness in the land seemed somehow to emanate from him. What Ariane did not know was that the King had been watching her, troubled by the aloof princess, determined to have her too, to take her bright youth before she could turn Elaan from him.

King Ingol invited Ariane and Elaan to stay at his castle. Their parents were delighted, thinking that the King wanted to choose Ariane as his bride, and, quite properly, had asked for Elaan as chaperone.

Ariane agreed, determined to protect Elaan no matter what.

The King was urbane and charming at table, clearly enjoying his guests. He provided them with wine and with rare sweetmeats, entertaining them with poems and stories. Then he asked Elaan to play an air, and Ariane to dance, which they did. Then, as the night wore on, he yawned and showed Elaan and Ariane to their chambers. Ariane followed him back to the great hall.

May I speak with you frankly?

Yes, my lovely Ariane.

I know that you desire my brother's bright youth. I offer myself in his place, if you will agree and will send him home tonight.

The King laughed. I will have both! he said, since we are being frank with one another. And he leapt upon Ariane and tore the clothes from her body, laughing as she fought him, and he took the princess Ariane's bright youth. He left her unconscious on the carpet and went to Elaan's chamber.

The King took Elaan's bright youth and cast him, grey and broken, into the forest.

Ariane awoke alone in the great hall. She gathered her clothes. She could sense that Elaan was long gone. She slipped down to the stables where she found Elaan's horse Fireas that had been Ingol's horse but loved Elaan as much as she had hated her former master. Ariane whispered to Fireas in words that only horses understand and dragged her aching and bruised body up onto the horse's bare back.

Ariane rode into the forest and neither she nor Elaan were seen again.

Ingol did not know that you cannot take from a visionary without giving something. The greater the theft, the bigger the gift. Ariane took a long while to recover but when she did, she was more powerful than Ingol could have imagined. She found Elaan quickly with the help of Fireas and healed him in secret, and the two became as loving as they had been before Ingol ever came to their castle. She became a spirit of the wind, and he a spirit of fire.

Ingol continued as he always had, taking what he wanted from the children of the surrounding lands.

One night a shining warrior and a strange princess knocked at Ingol's castle. They were invited in and put up in the same chambers as Ariane and Elaan had occupied many years before. After dinner, the warrior played the timbor and the princess danced. Neither had bright youth, but they were strange and beautiful, and Ingol was enchanted. He smiled and sang.

Who are you, strangers from a strange land? They didn't answer, but played harder and danced with greater wildness. The princess danced near and he thought he heard, whispered on the wind, Ariane and Elaan. Ingol leapt up, suddenly afraid, but then the whirling princess was upon him.

A whirlwind dropped King Ingol's dead body in the village square that night and his castle burned to the ground. The greyness lifted and slowly left that land altogether and the people thereafter worshipped the whirlwinds and fire.

This was Lilo's favourite story and for a while Ursula liked telling it. Then she forgot it altogether.

'All's well that ends well,' Pa said. The morning storm was over and the children were tired and ready for school, only delayed by half an hour this time. He beamed at his lanky children. They scowled back. Pa could make any one of them laugh, melt, smile, twist away in shy adolescent happiness.

Pa jollied them into the car and smoothed their ragged feelings. 'She won't let me eat *lettuce*,' he whispered once they were on the highway, rolling his eyes.

They were silent but smiled, staring out the window so he wouldn't get them too easily.

'She won't let me eat cabbage,' he said, turning round and wobbling on the road as he raised his hands palm up level with his ears and gripped the steering wheel between his big knees.

The kids laughed and shrieked, 'Watch the ROAD!'

'No sauerkraut for me and no *sauces* on no *sau-au-au-au-sage*,' Pa sang in an operatic tenor.

'No *toilet* paper for my bottom, no *toothpaste* for my teeth,' sang Siegfried.

'No underpants and no overcoats, no right sleeves, no left legs,' shrieked Helmut.

'No sesame, no sesame, no sesame, NO NO NO SESAME in my supreme soufflé,' sang Gotthilf, and the car veered and swung with their laughter.

They arrived at school, and alighted dishevelled and suddenly serious once the car doors opened.

But sometimes Pa, too, got depressed and huddled in dull confusion, deserted by his optimism. Some genial spirit left him and he sat in bleak emptiness, waiting for it to return and whisper reassurances in his ear. Pa's self became draughty. He avoided Acantia and the children avoided him. He sat in the closed auditorium tuning the viola over and over again. Eventually he began playing scales, children's exercises, Wohlfart's Viola Exercises, then tricky fragments of pieces and then viola parts of Haydn quartets, then whole sonatas, playing for ten hours in the closed auditorium. The children listened in with one ear as their universe was, poco a poco, rebuilt and set to rights.

By the time Gotthilf was sixteen, going to school had become a grim ritual with Acantia in which they all sensed she was powerless to do more than harry. Acantia sent them to school abraded and late. Breakfast was rhubarb, wheatgerm, brewer's yeast, dolomite, junket and freshly vitamised silverbeet and apple juice. Gotthilf threw up into the bracken and ixodia nearly every morning as he trudged through the clay cutting to the main road and the school bus. If breakfast wasn't downed on time to catch the school bus or to get a ride with Pa, Acantia made them eat it when they got home.

Lunches were unpresentable at school. In Acantia's world they were not only healthy but also quite tasty. In the world of school, Gotthilf risked having his head held down the toilet with his garlic, homemade cheese and Acantia-bread lunch swilling around his face if he dared even carry it out of Acantia land. He was caught after Acantia found his discarded lunch on the side of the bush track.

A boy who doesn't need his lunch doesn't need his dinner.

Acantia beat Gotthilf every day when he came home from school. It ceased to matter why. If he had done nothing wrong, crimes were ruthlessly engineered. The barrier between the permitted and the forbidden was moved in the night without his knowledge. Gotthilf stopped trying to be good. Ursula, who also went to school, knew Acantia had to be right. She wanted Acantia to be right.

Gotthilf was beaten twice most days because by the time Pa stopped practising and came to join the family for the evening, he would be past caring.

Acantia exclaimed tiredly, 'I don't know what to do! Pa, I am at my wits' end! The boy is sick. I cannot discipline him. His *father* will have to do something! Look at him! He's a muttering slouch. He comes home from school with that terrible look on his face. God only knows what goes on there, but a face like that tells all!'

Pa went to see Gotthilf, to exact contrition, with Acantia behind his shoulder.

Gotthilf laughed an evil, adult, King John laugh.

'I will never apologise to that that . . . that . . .!'

'Aah!' Acantia gasped, as if punched. 'Hit him! Hit him! It's the only thing he understands!'

Pa beat Gotthilf. He never thought that delinquency and the tortured sense of injustice might look the same. But Acantia just said sadly, 'Gotthilf has had a splinter of ice in his heart since he was a baby.'

Gotthilf quietly collected and labelled swear words and pejorative or derogatory phrases. He was the Delinquent, after all. He was also greedy for knowledge of the outside. He knew the meaning and etymology of *pash, screw, cunt, hard-on, fuck, box, bush, friggin', jerk-off, wanker, poofter, pansy, boong, nip, nigger, bloody*. It was Gotthilf who tried to clear up Siegfried's notion of the meaning of poofter.

'Poofters are NOT a brand of motorbike.'

But Siegfried needed more than a delinquent's word to be convinced.

Gotthilf stared down at the mud already covering Trevor's runners and wriggled his chilblains inside them, trying to stop his heart beating too fast. The mean rain of Toggenberg winter slanted through the trees and soaked into the thirty-two shivering boys waiting in the open for the start of the interschool cross-country. 'Get 'em dirdy, Goddo, an' I'll skin ya. Come to think of it, lose in my runners an' I'll skin ya,' Trevor had said. Gotthilf had won every cross-country in Berg, scampering cheekily to the finishing line minutes ahead of even the matric boys. Teachers whispered together about a Berg win in the interschool, and even a win in the state, in the open competition.

From the shelter sheds came muffled, half-hearted pep-ups from cold schoolmates and spine-stiffeners from competitive parents. Gotthilf hadn't told Acantia of the race. He knew Ursula was in the shed somewhere, but wished she wasn't.

Gotthilf glanced from under his dripping fringe at the other competitors. Unfriendly, unfamiliar boys in unfamiliar uniforms. Jumping to keep warm, stretching. Professional schoolboys. He stared quickly back at his goose-pimpled red arms. He felt a wave of horror. He had caught the look on some of their faces. Excitement. Energy. Competence. Hatred. His heart began racing in a kind of terror as they were called up for the start and he almost fainted as they waited those last sickening seconds. He was going to fail. 'Omi God, Omi God, Omi God, Goddo!' The chant sounded frail under the tin sheds and the rain. A voice came, sodden, unfamiliar, 'Killem, Goddo!'

He started badly. The track narrowed quickly to a single trail along a fence line and boys jostled and shoved in the liquid clay, slipping and stumbling. Gotthilf, the smallest, got bounced and jostled to near the back of the pack. He pounded the sludge, wiping the mud thrown from the two boys ahead of him from his eyes. The rain was pouring down now in cold streamers. Five thousand metres, maybe a little less, to go. He had no cheeky, inexhaustible spring of energy, nothing. His legs seemed to be made of a doll's wire and rubber, not flesh and bone. They bent unpredictably as they took his weight and had to be straightened with effort to take it again.

The mud splashed up his legs and into his shorts. He could feel its grit clasp his balls and ride up his belly. Each step seemed to take him deeper, each splash to grip him with greater viscosity, greater power. He warmed slowly, running half in a dream world. He suddenly imagined the earth's hands reaching for him to pull him into the dead goat's grave, but it was no idle scary thought. Something in him had switched on and he stumbled in terror, his legs dissolving. The grit rose to cloak his eyelashes and he screamed with every breath. Each sucking step pulled his leg and held and he fought, certain now that he could feel hands, mouths in the mud, certain that it had him and would never let him go. Then he fell, suddenly, arms too slow to save him, and he went face first into the track. At the last awful moment he turned his face to the side and was left buried in the mud with one eye to the soaking rain and his nose submerged in heavy clinging clay. He screamed as he sucked in panic for air, and pushed against the seemingly bottomless mud, reaching, inching slowly for a handhold. He managed to push himself out and away with all the strength he could find. The liquid earth gave him up with a sucking sound and a wet sigh. He stumbled on. The track lifted from the lowlands and into the bush. The stringybark leaves slap-slapped in the rain with a welcome solid sound.

He was alone now in the bush, sliding and skating the slicked track, using his hands to scrape the mud off his shuddering body. He began to weep in the aftermath and from exhaustion, and in the knowledge of shame and humiliation to come.

Gotthilf ran long last. He arrived at the sodden knoll of the finishing line sobbing so openly that everyone looked away. A teacher put arms around him and that made it worse. But even as his sobs poured from his wrung-out muddy body, something in him sat still and clear-eyed, drumming with the thought, *I will never do or be this again.*

The Berg boys were silent on the bus back to school.

Gotthilf redeemed himself with Acantia for a day. He went on a school excursion to Berg Cliffs, discovering along the way that Trevor's family were Ramindjeri and that Trevor couldn't swim. Both pieces of information put him into a high pressure state of happiness. He pestered Trevor for titbits of Ramindjeri history and of Trevor's fascinatingly miserable childhood in foster homes. He felt himself swell with skill, knowledge and power. His dives and water displays had an edge to them, a demonstration of prowess, and Trevor was uncomplicatedly admiring.

When a woman leapt into the foam to save her drowning ten year old, and when her desperate efforts began to fail in the hidden rip, Gotthilf already felt like a giant and didn't hesitate. He was a superb swimmer. He dived in, swam strongly out to the boy, trod water as he wrenched the flailing child around and pulled an arm up tight between his shoulderblades. Then Gotthilf hugged him in close and hissed, 'Don't squirm or I'll accentuate,' demonstrating viciously what he meant. The boy wailed as he spluttered, and hid rather than thank his rescuer once on the beach. The mother managed to swim ashore, once she saw that her boy was in good hands.

Gotthilf was a hero. Even Trevor said so. The teacher clapped him on the back and told him he was a fine lad.

Acantia was very surprised. 'Just goes to show that good blood and upbringing will out, no matter the company one keeps.' She smiled and shook her head in wonder. 'When the going gets tough, the true character shines.' She hugged Gotthilf close while Ursula looked on with envy. Buoyed by bliss, Gotthilf told his story over and over again. Acantia made a hero's roast chicken for dinner, with carrots and potatoes and lettuce salad. Beate, Ursula and Lilo sang a song, ranged behind his chair, in his honour. Ursula longed for something terrible to happen right in front of her nose so she too could show what she was made of.

The next day Acantia's mood was grim. Gotthilf beamed at her and got no response. She gave his school uniform a leaden stare and went back to bed. When he got home from school it was all over.

'Sit down,' she said, tight-lipped. 'I rang your teacher, that weak man Mr Quinn, and I spoke to Mrs Poulos, the New Australian woman you say you rescued, and the surf life saving club. There were no high waves, you rescued one, not two people. You probably got in the way of the surf lifesavers, the proper men for the job, and almost caused Mrs Poulos and her son to drown.' Her eyes blasted him and she screamed in his face, 'You pathetic, corrupt little liar! Until you leave those filthy degraded friends, don't ever pass your defiled words in my hearing!'

Gotthilf sat, small and pale. Bitter as his heart became, he could not keep silent. He took to strafing the kitchen with vile words and then running.

Ursula was delighted. With Gotthilf out of the race, she had a chance at being the good one.

School became a bad daydream. Acantia's world was crumbling and throughout their school years the younger Houdinis trickled in and out of schools. They were tortured at school.

Gotthilf was caught shoplifting underpants. Acantia sent him to a psychologist to humiliate him.

'Children, gather round. Gotthilf is infected with the mental diseases of this society. He is a Liar and a Delinquent, yes. But he has sunk lower. He is a Thief. He has chosen the path of degradation and criminality. There is very little more I can do for him. But I will not under any circumstances let the same happen to any of you. I will stamp it out at the first sign. I know now what to look for.'

Gotthilf ran away from home after knocking Acantia out.

He covered the walls of his caravan with texta graffiti.

'No wuckin' furries. NO WUCKIN' FURRIES! NO WUCKIN' FURRIES!' and, 'MOTHER-F-FFF!'

He was still quite a small boy. He was a weedy seventeen, with a cheeky grin and a flinch.

They all agreed for a while that he had done a terrible thing and would rue it all his days.

Acantia was tormenting Gotthilf and he said something no one could later recall. She went to swipe his face with the pressure cooker lid and he ducked and pushed her hard against the stove top. She crumpled and lay on the floor with her eyes shut. Gotthilf was deathly pale. They all stared, paralysed. It was as if a bomb was falling in front of them and everything had slowed to nightmare time. Gotthilf stood leaning against the chair, his hair standing out like a halo around his white face. Pa was down on the floor shaking Acantia.

Lilo walked in and took in the scene. She said matter-of-factly, '*Gotthilf!* I reckon you've killed her!'

Beate slapped Lilo with all her might across the face and then burst into tears. Lilo nursed her cheek glowering and muttered sotto voce, 'Only joking! Jeez! I didn't know he *really* had!'

Acantia suddenly sat up and looked around brightly. She laughed and stared into Gotthilf's eyes.

'Scared ya!' she said, her voice shaky and mirthless, and jumped up.

Gotthilf packed his stolen underwear, socks, shoes, shirts, yet-to-be-worn jeans, matches, pocketknife, aftershave and bow resin into his stolen backpack.

'Conflagrate in hell,' he whispered, looking back across the still grasses of the moonlit weed ocean that stretched from the house to the bush. The moonlight made a glacier inch through the grass. Then a wind gust melted it all in a frenzy of glittering eddies. The grasses sighed. He stepped over the sagging boundary fence, elated, wide-eyed, clammy.

Pa visited Gotthilf occasionally in secret but his brothers and sisters barely saw him again. Acantia acted as though he had never existed. Gotthilf and Acantia never forgave each other. It was true love between them: betrayal hurt forever. Ursula tried not to miss her delinquent brother. Ursula was a little jealous, always, of Gotthilf.

Arno was a very quiet kid. He spoke his own language, which they all learned, until he was four or five. Arno played chess with anyone he could trap into it. He hovered at the fringes of family storms and battles with the board and pieces tucked under his arm. As soon as he had someone in his sights, he could draw and lay out the pieces with the speed of a gunslinger. Being beaten at chess by Arno was like reading on the toilet. It was time out from ordinary life, since Acantia would not interrupt a chess game, although she would ask Arno to make the kill quickly if necessary.

Arno kept five clocks going in the house, and telephoned the time regularly to check them against each other. The auditorium had Paris time, the kitchen Toggenberg time, the kids' room London time, the cuckoo clock in Beate's house Berlin time; and the time he kept on his watch was a secret.

When Arno was thirteen they discovered that he was deaf, having narrow ear canals which were almost permanently swollen and blocked with wax. However, by then everyone was so used to his deaf personality that it was disturbing whenever he had his canals washed out and became someone else. He began to pretend to be deaf in order to fit in.

Arno didn't know it, but he was monochrome-sighted. He could only see blue. Standing behind Lilo on Ash Wednesday and holding Acantia's hand, Arno watched his sister's hair extended to the sky by flames on the hilltop behind her head. The hair, the flames and the sky were one. Fire was so beautiful. It was like the sweet, faint music he could sometimes hear. Fire was all the colours of the rainbow, a symphony of merging and harmonising tones. He wished everything would burn. Behind him the dam glistened like a cow's eye. Dam water was never blue, he knew. It was blue he was waiting for, straining his ears for. Sky and eye blue. Orange was the most bluish part of flame.

The sky was Arno's certainty, on a clear day. He loved blue, and the real sky was always blue. His eyes travelled upward to a zenith, from which he could anchor his world.

Arno controlled his world by remembering the days. All his energy was taken up with a mantric recitation running continuously in his head. He knew the weather, the weekday and the salient events for every date going back to his third birthday, and before that was chaos. They were catalogued and cross-referenced, memorised and maintained like a garden. The weeds from any day could start spreading to their surrounding weeks, some could jump years, once the layers thickened. Revisiting his days and weeding them of the events that belonged elsewhere made him slow at school because it was a full-time job. But he was more reliable than a calendar, and his days could be called on to resolve disputes and to find things that had been lost. The days were the key to order.

He did not like events that seemed to take more than one day to finish. The fire was very satisfactory.

Acantia once called Lilo the *all-gold girl*, but Arno could easily imagine her blue. Krishna blue, especially when she had a suntan and was sweaty. Was her blood really red like other people's? He had sometimes stared at his own in private, watching a trickle run down his arm, almost sure that, with no one else around, it was winking from red to blue. Lilo once walked in on him and screamed and the pool on the floor flicked back to red instantly. Lilo kept his colours in place.

Arno loved what came from his body. He treasured his hair and his earwax. In spring he let birds take his hairs from the roof of his caravan and spent all summer tracking which nests he'd helped build. He never made Secret Spots. Something secret was coming from inside him and it was almost certainly blue.

Another winter battered Whispers, the rain blasting through the bush to the sound of slapping gum leaves. The ground was sodden, pungent with black beetles. Only around the house the pines and firs sighed, an oasis of whispering voices, ghosts from elsewhere. Beate's violin sang out from a candlelit room, notes of silent snowfall, of the long dark and the doona-covered world of northern winter, of the eerie deadly comfort of a blanket of snow. Beate knew she would go. As soon as she could fly, she would follow the magnetic songlines rising from the maple child cradled in her hands. She longed for the warmth of snow and the children she could love if she were far enough away.

Ursula and Acantia crept along in the undergrowth, treading carefully to avoid crackling kindling underfoot.

'Shhh,' whispered Acantia, turning to Ursula with a mime's elaborate movements. Her arm and hand made a scroll before her finger unfurled and came to her lips. Ursula grinned and mimicked her exactly but unfurled her finger at the last minute to pick her nose.

Acantia snuffled with suppressed laughter. She pointed ahead and they both crouched down, peering through a bank of broom. The animal they had been stalking had stopped still and could not be seen clearly. Its furry form could be made out dimly. They froze, sensing that it had seen them. Ursula's heart pounded. It had a lumbering, brownish, woolly form. They had followed it for about twenty metres, alternately dashing and freezing, keeping downwind.

Suddenly it burst through the broom and hit Acantia full lob in the chest, roaring. Acantia went down under it and, her mind writhing, Ursula leapt on top of it, clenching great fistfuls of its hair. Its huge pelt came off in her hands and she fell backwards into the broom with the massive skin on top of her. She struggled frantically out from under it, hearing Acantia making a strange noise. The animal sounded as though it was eating her mother in gulps. She leapt up. Acantia was lying in the brush next to Helmut. Both of them were laughing, tears coursing down their cheeks.

All three of them lay on the underbrush and laughed themselves quiet, staring at the blue sky through the trees. A currawong whistled and klonged. Ursula answered.

Then silence. Then listening to insects.

'Ouch,' said Acantia.

'Hopper ant,' said Helmut.

But none of them moved.

Beate played. Her fingers flew, their stumps raw. Her fingerprints had long ago been worn away. Her violin, crushed under her chin, was the frail love child of ebony and maple. Beate screamed and howled with its voice. The smell of hot resin and the fine white powder rising in slow motion from her flashing bow were in her nostrils.

Beate played scales like a caged tiger.

But when she played herself beyond her known world she felt her heart swelling, bursting, the hot blood drenching the violin along with her sweat and with the ooze from the suppurating sore on her chin. Her body and her senses soared, crying out for love and protection. Her music sang of her mother's arms about her, of her arms about a child and her hot whisper that would heal all:

I love you, love you, love you to the ends of the earth and the end of time.

Ursula sat outside, pounding clay to remove the air bubbles before sculpting. Beate ripped through the Devil's Trill like a locomotive, then suddenly hit the grief of a wide valley, filled with rivers, forests, snow-covered spruces, loneliness and loss. Ursula looked up, her breath caught and held in the strings when Beate stopped. Silence sizzled around them both and Ursula could hear her sister gasping inside the room.

The children sat around the dinner table, silent. Whenever evening fell and the uncertain flicker of the fluoro lit the kitchen, something sad seemed to settle at the table with them. The lighting was yellow, the shadowed corners daunting. The Tarsinis were ranged in the dim window, their heads in their palms, lank hair also flicked over brows, elbows either side of their empty bowls. The fluoro picked up a dull shine from the walls and the fire died down to embers. No one moved. Beate looked strained and Lilo's eyes were flicking from face to face for answers. They all had the quiet-breathing rigidity of dogs with ears pricked. Acantia was howling outside in the rain, her voice emitted in time lapse snatches, tracking her sprint through the cow paddock, the orchard, and then faintly from the bush rim. Then she fell silent and the children's spines tensed as if they had all drawn breath. They waited, each looking to the others for signs. They waited long minutes. Suddenly Acantia burst in the door, breathing hard and smiling ecstatically. Her hair was black and slick, plastered in tendrils to her white forehead, her lips red. Her eyes were wild and shining. She was shaken suddenly by a storm of sobs, her smile tightening to a grimace. She doubled over. The children smiled uncertainly, hopefully, without relaxing. Acantia flung herself upright, her hair spraying the ceiling and walls from its black points. She threw an ardent look to her children.

'I have been communing!' she breathed.

She hugged each of them and went to bed. The children listened until they heard her door close and her bed creak and then Beate rose carefully and with almost noiseless motions made them all a dinner of fried rice, eggs and silverbeet. Lilo looked at Ursula across the table.

'Will we ever be better?'

Ursula's face was pale, her eyes dark and worried.

'Eat your food and shut up.'

Lilo looked relieved.

Beate, Ursula and Lilo sang madrigals and rounds, standing gazing at nothing in the centre of the auditorium. Their singing voices filled the room, knocking up against the walls, ringing through the paintings into the depths of Schwarzwald, of Luzerne, of snowfall and out faintly to the dim bush perimeter.

Beate's descant rose high in flight over the sad chords of the round. Beate was, one day, going home.

The sweet voices of the three sisters calling for the forest and Beate's lost love:

Alles Schweiget
Nachtigalen
Locken mit Süssen
Melodien
Tränen ins Auge
Schwermut ins Herz

Ziggy and Ursa riffled through the glossy catalogue of Acantia's Great Exhibition. Acantia's Great Exhibition had come as a surprise in every way. Pa had long ceased giving concerts and public appearances. Acantia had declined all official invitations on his behalf so effectively that gilt-edged letters to A Hartmut Houdini were a thing of the past. Acantia had shone all week with a fierce delight, and giggled at their open mouths when she slammed the catalogue down onto the table.

Ursula had accepted unquestioningly that the problem was with the public, not with Pa. As she looked at the catalogue, she could hear Pa practising. For the first time she heard and noted the meaning of the rough, sobbing notes, out of pitch. There was a garish, raw grief in his playing. Beate was practising too, further away. Pa's notes were embarrassing sliding tears against that crystal desire. She tried to catch Siegfried's eye, but he wasn't looking or listening.

The catalogue was an unexpectedly authentic looking document, printed with a beautiful font on fine paper, embellished with ornamental scrollwork and quotes from the artist. The paintings were reproduced in stunning colour. Ursula and Siegfried turned the pages slowly, feeling with their fingertips the independence of the image conferred by photographic reduction. The paintings had grown wings and soared away. They were minute in their altitude and distance. They were familiar and transformed. They were Acantia's children, born from her eye, flying away.

The back cover said: *With seven colours I can make the world.* Acantia.

Cadmium Yellow, Cadmium Red, Prussian Blue, Titanium White, Cerulean Blue and Vandyke Brown. Ursula could only ever count six but she was forgetting the one which is an absence and sits waiting on the masonite.

The catalogue gave a biography of Acantia. She was born with paintbrush in hand, it said. She was married to the famous viola player A Hartmut Houdini. She had seven brilliant children. They all lived together in a house in the bush awash with the colours of the several artists in the clan and ringing with the music of a string quartet, a trio and a bassoon. Dawn to dusk her life was Love, Hope, Music, Faith and Creativity.

It said she was studying for her doctorate in Poona University, India, in Ayurvedic Medicine and that her painting reflected a philosophy of supreme health and physical and psychic completion.

She was the author of numerous books on Art and Therapy, Shells and Therapy and Canine Phrenology and, under a pseudonym, was a health columnist for the local newspaper. They laughed a little at some of her comments. She had written assessments for each painting.

> *This is a selfish painting, but none the worse for that. It is painted purely for the pleasure of the artist but here that can give pleasure too.*

They came to a page from which a painting leapt renewed. It was a huge picture, nearly filling a wall of their house. It had become the wall and everyone had ignored it for years. It had vanished some weeks before, and they had all stood staring in gob-smacked wonder at the clean-if-cobwebby square it had left behind. 'It is a thing of . . . great beauty,' Helmut had said. 'Art in the purest sense.' They shrieked in laughter and never bothered to ask where the painting was. Other paintings had disappeared too. For a while, every time they passed the blank walls, they pretended to be gripped, inspired or critical.

It is a painting of the bush track that leads to the neighbours' house. A winding path, alternately lit and shadowed. Great swathes of colour (blue, green, yellow, blue-black) hang in the air, suggesting with their solidity the delicacy and evanescence of the moment.

Acantia had written at the end of her technical commentary: *The path is uninviting. We prefer to stay at home.*

Siegfried turned the page to a painting of the house viewed from above.

The house is a tiny pinkish blob with a vacant staring window and a coil of smoke ascending from the chimney. It is embedded, obscured by Prussian blue radiata pines and layers of field and forest in the colours of a late summer tinder haze. The pines in the foreground seem black, and the sandy green and dull red of the gums is brittle and dry. There is no sky.

The painting emerged from the print clearer than on the wall. Acantia had scrubbed off the browning haze of fly specks in the bathtub before the exhibition. Ursula and Ziggy pored over this painting. On the facing page Acantia had written:

This was clearly an emotional subject for the artist. The loving brushwork and the detail of the framing landscape all centre on the little home nestled in these beautiful hills. We can sense the harmony and peace of life in this place. Down there, we can tell, creative and good things are happening. It is a warm beating heart, the centre of the artist's world.

Ursula and Ziggy stared at each other in delight. They snorted and rocked and spluttered. Ziggy hesitated only for a moment and then drew a little lighted fuse from the smoking house on the catalogue.

'Nuclear family!' Ziggy said.

Ursula was looking at the catalogue, alone. What colour am I? The thought rolled lazily about in her mind. Arno was blue, cerulean blue and Lilo was yellow, everyone could see that. She liked the adjectives, not the nouns. Titanium. Prussian. Cadmium. Vandyke.

She stared at a forest which had no density, made only from impressions of the weave of the world. All colours were somehow spun and stretched into broad verticals and horizontals and yet it was a forest. But the bush and the trees around the house were not real in the pictures. A prickling absence wrapped around her, as if floating in the sea, staring up and then suddenly feeling as though the deep extends forever behind the skull. Everything light and bright was talking ceaselessly, muttering sotto voce of darkness. She stared at the catalogue, mist descending. She started to sweat and wanted to shut the pages but she could not stop staring. Something was wrong with the world, their world. Pa was no longer a musician. Acantia was the centre now and Acantia preferred to stay at home. Home. Home. She could not bear it.

Acantia's stringybarks were too fat, too benign. They blended too smoothly, too concordantly, with their world. Light and shadow fell across one painting in spectacularly geometric assurance. Acantia had not recorded the hostility of light, the independent, aloof grey of stringybarks; their lean, hungry scramble and the scars of survival. She perhaps had not remarked that the shade of a radiata pine has a menacing look, and yet it managed to menace through the painting despite her. As Ursula stared at the beautiful painting, she had a vision.

The house's mouth opened and roared red and black and voracious around her head. Acantia's lips were stretched in a scream at the edge of Ursula's vision. Acantia's eyes loomed over that strange rim. Ursula's head was in a black, roaring tunnel. A voice said, pleading, 'But I love you!'

'There is something wrong with Acantia,' she whispered out loud. And she suddenly felt rather than remembered how often she had had that thought and had suppressed it.

She was crying softly, longing for numb confusion, for mountain fog. She wanted the house destroyed and the vicious white light let in.

She was sixteen.

Newkiller Family became the name of Siegfried's goat circus and that summer's number one joke.

Acantia stood still and silent in the centre of the squalid kitchen. The fridge door was open, pouring its cold rot smells into the fetid atmosphere. The window was closed, sealed shut now for two years. A bucket was overturned at Acantia's feet and yoghurt was spread across the kitchen like icing or a paint bomb. The violence of its fall was clear from the height of the white spatter on the walls. The lemon stink of yoghurt rose as it slowly seeped down through clothes, papers, old dishes, feathers, hair, bones and dust to the floor. Acantia watched it settle, her face blank. She didn't notice Ursula watching from the porch door. She seemed to shrink, something trickling down her spine and draining away. She turned and walked back into the auditorium.

Ursula stood a long while, as blank as her mother, then turned too and walked back outside.

That was the quiet end of all Ursula's cleaning.

abendmusik

Beate had become a pretty and dreamy girl with sapphire blue eyes and a hairstyle created by some secret implements unknown to her sisters.

It was from Beate's cache that Ursula first filched sanitary napkins. Sanitary napkins were a dangerous commodity to have in one's possession. Acantia occasionally humiliated her daughters by ripping through their things, screaming, 'Show me your rags!' Beate and Ursula were supposed to rip up old sheets. Beate stood red, silent and rebellious when she was held up as an example. She was eighteen and had developed a workable way of measuring whether or not Acantia was right or wrong. Old sheets and menstrual blood stank: Acantia was wrong.

Tampons were only used after leaving Acantia's world. At Whispers they were spoken of with a slightly lowered voice, for a girl who used them was not a real virgin. To be caught in flagrante with a tampon was a horror not to be contemplated.

Dealing with used sanitary napkins (or unsanitary sheets) was difficult. They were supposed to burn them but the kitchen and especially the fireplace were prohibitively public places. Putting them in the garbage was also fraught with shaming dangers. If wrapped in toilet paper, they were conspicuous and wasteful and likely to arouse curiosity or ire. Burying them took a great deal of planning and a dog deterrent. Stashing them in some out of the way place was disastrous. Ursula got to the stage where she couldn't see blood on anyone or anything, even fresh, without wondering if it wasn't somehow issuing from her, or was the trail leading to her crimes, laid by the house to trap her.

Beate was lucky. She could bundle them up in her handbag and drop them into an ordinary, anonymous bin in the city on her way to uni.

Beate had become a great violinist. Her hands were never large enough to become a violist but at some point in her eighteenth year she stopped wishing for a different body. Her body sang on the metal lines running from her chin to the vanishing point at her fingers and she dreamed of riding the trans-Siberian railroad through vast snowfields. The metal lines shone under the arch of her flying fingers, vibrating through her body, through her feet down into the earth to where the lava lies. She stared down the tracks to the tunnel under her fingers. That, so close, was the way out. Beate gave concerts when she was eighteen and they said in the papers that she was a lady Menuhin.

Beate won prize after prize, finally winning a scholarship to study with the violin master Duro Elenis.

The Houdinis went wild with joy. Beate sat smiling quietly as her brothers and sisters whirled around her.

She wandered outside, adjusting to being outside for the first time. She looked at the house and at the paddocks, thinking. *There, I once played. There I once was Beate Houdini*. She looked at the first pine tree and imagined it cut down and carted away for firewood. She would wave it off with an appropriate show of regret and inner satisfaction. She waved her arm at the dark and sombre tree. Her brothers and sisters pelted from the house, shrieking over something or other. She would miss them, she thought happily. It would be such a pleasure to miss them. She sat with her back to the wall of the kitchen, watching them tumble in the grass like puppies. Acantia's and Pa's voices rose in the room behind her.

'We'll have to crate some of the paintings to take with her to make it feel like home. It will only be three months a year, and with her mother by her side . . .'

Pa murmured something.

'Yes, a true Houdini.'

Beate sat at the edge of her bed feeling as if a lead weight was pulling her through the mattress and down into the dank earth underneath the house. She was white in the face, staring down at her hands. They were clean and fine. Athletic hands. Her left was different from her right, noticeably larger. It had tough pads at the fingertips, hardened from the long journey on that cruel steel and gut. No fingerprints. The floor was spread with newspaper clippings, black and white photos of her Lady Di cut above her lost and longing eyes, her chin crooked over the chinrest and the four steel tracks blurred in the print.

TOGGENBERG BEAUTY SHOWS REAL TALENT

DOING THE HOUDINIS PROUD, TOGGENBERG'S VIOLINIST ESCAPES TO GERMANY

OH YOU BEAUTY, BEATE! HOUDINI WINS AGAIN

In one photo Acantia and Pa beam into the camera, Acantia crushing Beate in an embrace. Acantia has food on her cheek and forehead.

Beate looked out of the window where she had once watched the man chop Radha up. She picked up her bankbook and hid it under the floorboards where no one would find it. She walked out the door, past the deodar and the apple, and over to the woodpile. She laid her left hand, palm up, on the pitted block. She stared at the curling fingers, her hand as usual holding the neck of an invisible violin. She could see the violin and knew, coldly, that it was just wood and strings.

She swung the axe proficiently and dispassionately with her right hand, as if chopping small wood.

Two fingers and a fingertip curled in the woodchips like fat blue worms.

When Beate got out of hospital, she and Pa and Acantia were very quiet. A pall hung over everyone and the house was relatively spotless.

'It was a terrible accident,' Acantia said, many times over, but she eyed her daughter with something new in her eyes. To Beate it looked like fear.

'You are a violinist. Why did you chop wood? That was Ursula's job.' Then she said, tears in her eyes, 'What will you be now? Maybe you can still become a poet. Oh Beate, that was a silly silly *silly* thing to do!'

But Acantia also left her alone after that, too shocked to harry her. Acantia began to look at her daughter as if she couldn't recognise her.

Ursula slunk about, believing that it was her fault. She had begun to prefer things to be her fault. It simplified everything and gave effort meaning. Acantia helped give the convoluted argument of Ursula's guilt some truth by interacting with her at a minimum and throwing her the occasional malevolent glance. Ursula stayed out of her mother's way and spent sleepless nights whispering *sorry sorry sorry* to the dark ceiling. She spent her days avoiding being in the same room as Beate or Acantia, but trailing them.

Beate didn't seem to hold a grudge against her sister or her mother. She was white and silent. She had a bag packed under her bed with one change of clothes and the two remaining leaves of *The Tomten*.

Two months later Beate walked out with her pack in one hand and her bandaged arm in a sling and caught the train to Melbourne; then, a short time later, a plane to Germany.

Ursula guessed before anyone else did that Beate had done it on purpose.

Ursula could hear Acantia sobbing behind the closed door of her room, but all her mother said to the kids was, 'She never could face the vicissitudes of life with humour. Talk about overreacting.'

No one knew for sure what she was talking about. Beate settled into Germany somehow. None of them could imagine how, so Beate ceased to be real to them. She was a collection of facts, now. They had never read Beate's prose before, so her voluminous letters with their breathless, ardent style were the letters of a stranger. An architecture student in Freiburg, Germany. Gone to the land of paintings and memories. They remembered the violinist, and the ghost of her playing haunted them. It was a shock to see that she was stump-handed and big-bellied, smiling an unfamiliar smile in her wedding photos.

Ursula missed her bitterly. With Beate and Gotthilf gone, she was the eldest. She felt a heavy cloak settle on her shoulders. She looked at Helmut, Siegfried, Lilo and Arno and knew that they had become her responsibility. She sat alone in her caravan watching the huntsman spiders conduct their affairs as if even they were already a memory and felt the heaviness of a cold truth squeeze her tight. *For her crimes, she would pay*. They were her responsibility and the time for vacillation and childish fantasy was over. She too would be leaving, but not like the others. She would have to leave and somehow take the younger ones with her. *Thenceforth she had to keep the little ones from harm*. She felt cold and scared.

Then she felt excited. Her limbs filled with blood and her chest swelled with a sweet intake. She could not afford regret if she was to be a hero.

Leaving was, in the end, simple, a matter of walking away and not returning.

It took a while for Ursula to get around to it. At seventeen, having scraped through the matriculation public examination, she was lounging around the farm, looking like a delinquent, with a glowering expression and chopped greasy hair, and wishing she knew how to smoke properly. Acantia couldn't bear the sight of her, so when Ursula got an offer to study Arts at the University of Toggenberg, Acantia clocked her on the head with a waffle iron and said, 'Go, see if we care or need you here!' and Ursula washed her clothes for the first time that summer in a state of quiet excitement.

Three weeks later, against all expectations, she was at university, and Whispers ceased to exist from eight until six. Three weeks after that she was missing lectures and secretly meeting Speed, a fine-built boy whose skin had an aromatic, burning smell which she found out much later was Tiger Balm. He looked quite unlike a Houdini. For one thing he wasn't white.

Speed was pro everything but could argue anti anything better than anyone Ursula had ever encountered. She fell in love with him like a drowning tiger rescued, giddy, clutching on, bug-eyed with relief, frighteningly hungry.

But even starting university and gulping Speed down in long gasps saw her slinking home in the evenings, crawling back into her fetid bed with relief and frustration.

Then Acantia found out. Helmut saw them kissing in the savagery of parting, barely hidden in the scrub by the clay cutting, and told. Acantia beat her daughter with the broom handle and a saucepan.

'Just leave then! What makes you think I want you, you shambling shoddy slut-thing! Penis fodder! Pack! GET OUT!' Acantia was certain of Ursula's dependence, Ursula's love, Ursula's cowardice, and perhaps this alone drove Ursula to prove herself. 'Can't move?' Acantia heaved in dramatic parody of Ursula's gasping sobs, Ursula's shame. 'Go hang yourself! There's rope in the shed all prepared. Yes, do you think I don't know? That sentiment-sodden van of yours! Your sketches! I regret ever giving birth to a piece of sentimental trash like you!'

Acantia slammed the flimsy board that served as the house door. It broke, and she turned, kicking it to the ground in front of her. Ursula had sat heavily on a chair and had her head in her hands. Acantia screamed over her, 'And don't think anything comes without a price! It's so easy to give up, isn't it? Look at Beate. Look at G—that brother. Give up, Give up!' Acantia dropped her voice into the tones of a stern admonishment. 'You'll lose everything you have been given. Everything! I'll burn the lot, don't think I won't. And that will only be the beginning, because you'll lose your family. There will be no return!' She suddenly stamped through the debris at the doorway, pale and shaking, screaming, 'And fix this bugger-er-ised door!'

Ursula felt a stabbing in her chest. Acantia was crying, as she had cried after Beate left. Ursula stood up, dizzy, something singeing her brain and turning her cold. She could hear someone sobbing, and feel her chest heaving and creaking like a ship in a storm, her breath jetting from her as if from a bellows, but she felt utterly black and calm, floating. She walked in slow motion, with her scalp crawling, to her caravan. She picked up her most perfect bird skeleton, a nightjar, brass wire shining at the joints of the translucent wing bones. It was the most beautiful thing she owned. She packed it gently in toilet paper. She looked around the van but could not bring herself to take anything else.

She walked away, ignoring Ember's whinny from the paddock, her eyes averted. Lilo trailed after her.

'Where are you going?'

'Away.'

'Past the gate?'

'Yes.'

Lilo caught her breath.

'She'll kill the horse, Ursa!'

Ursula didn't reply.

'Will you come back?'

'No.'

Lilo wrapped her arms around Ursula, crying.

'Take me too! I can be yours!'

Ursula suddenly felt strong, momentarily sure. She unwound her sister from her neck and torso, and placed her hands on Lilo's shoulders in a stagy gesture. She felt as though she was a character in a book and that cheered her. She immediately began to cry, and was cheered also by having appropriate, touching tears of parting. Everything was just right and too unreal.

'Soon, Lilo. I'll get a good house first.'

Then, almost as a dreamy afterthought, even though she had planned and polished the phrase, she said, 'Stay away from Ugolini. Tell the others too. If he comes when Pa and Acantia are out, hide. Pretend no one's home.'

Ursula sent Lilo back down to the house, needing to be alone. She walked through the clay cutting, where just a few days before, Speed had parked his father's Ford Falcon on the disused side track, and she had torn and battered at his body to know more, and to forget. She walked past the top gate, and then turned and looked around. To one side the stringybarks glittered and slapped. The farm was invisible now, hidden behind the dark spires of the radiatas. The old gate hung awry, half shut, half open. Keeping nothing in or out. She looked at it, dizzy, her mind blank but scored with a kind of sizzling haze. The farm looked deserted. It was so long since a car had entered or left and there were no footprints except her own. Speed's tyre tracks stood out as if luminescent.

She walked, knowing that she would never return except, perhaps, after a long long time, as a detached, confident visitor.

That was the morning of Ash Wednesday. Ursula walked the twenty kilometres to Toggenberg town and behind her the hills lit up in farewell and burned for three days. Seven people died and countless animals. The hills reeked and smouldered for weeks.

Ursula had stood up, wriggled out, walked to town, and was sitting staring past Speed with wide, dry eyes. She was seeing the goats and the horse and all the vulnerable flesh and bone of her past exposed to Acantia. She knew the bushfire was out of control. Ursula had lit Acantia, dry tinder flaring with the rush of her leaving, winds sucked and swirling in the wake of her long walk down the hills and gorges.

She would go back if she could, but she knew that her past was burning, shrivelling and shrinking minute by minute. It was a conflagration, a pyre, a storm sweeping all away. She felt as if flames were streaming from behind her head, the hair of a demon. She would not look back. She fingered the fine skeleton in her lap. She held it up to Speed.

'I made this.'

She didn't know what to say. How could he know? In just six hours she had already grown too large to ever fit back through that little hole. It had been the pinprick of starlight from that side, but was a solid ball of cooling black charcoal from this.

No more goats. February 16, 1983, Siegfried wrote in his goat diary on Ash Wednesday, the day Ursula left home, the day Ember and the last of the goats burned to death.

Ursula rented a large, run-down house in town and collected injured and unwanted dogs, cats, cockatoos and Houdinis. It became the Houdini Halfway House, not quite as clean or organised as the house of an ordinary person but certainly halfway there.

Ursula spent more time in her first two years at university sneaking around in the bush at Whispers than studying, surprising an ecstatic Lilo with a bear hug by the chook shed, and melting at the glow Arno would give off at the sight of her. She had intended to stay away but had sneaked back to spy on her parents and her childhood before a week had passed. She was never tempted to return to live. She told herself that she was preparing the way for her brothers' and sister's eventual escape, that she was keeping an eye on them.

The collection of fugitive Houdinis was by design rather than by natural flow down a hill. Ursula terraced the pathway, planted and tended to the lures, and made sure that, when the time came, they would all fall off the mountain, roll down the pre-determined track in precise, pre-plotted moves, and plop, sobbing and excited, at her front door. Their beds were ready and the bubble fridge full. It was her project, and the preparations gave her pleasure for months.

It took some years, but eventually, one by one, Siegfried, Lilo and Arno came to live there; Arno first at fourteen, Siegfried when he was seventeen, Lilo at sixteen. They stayed until ready to face the world, one way or another.

The family was weakened, bleeding from cracks and rents. Acantia started each day beleaguered, shaken by the absences at the table. The normality of meals, the forced routine were fake, they could all tell. And Pa's viola sounded rough, raw, unpleasing. It was a bad time for the world outside to also come and find the Houdinis.

Acantia's fears for the moral safety of her children boiled over with the arrival of Tracy. Tracy said that terry towelling shorts were passé. Tracy sang, 'I'll be your pros-ti-tute whenever you want me-ee.'

Acantia took her literally and called her a toxic degenerate. Acantia said she was the incarnation of popular culture, of contemporary Australia.

Tracy put a small hand on her skinny hip and gyrated through some moves so suggestive that Acantia couldn't bear to have her children see them.

She was ten when the Houdinis first met her. No one was quite sure how she and Lilo had become friends. Tracy lived a half-hour's walk away, the other side of three gullies of dense bush. Acantia couldn't send her home for lunch all that easily. She sat with Lilo at the end of the table and whispered something in Lilo's ear. Both of them spluttered. Everyone stared, chewing mechanically, shoving forkloads into their mouths without taking their eyes off her, helping themselves to seconds by feel. Acantia put on her nicest voice and began to question Tracy.

Tracy was happy to discuss then and there:

a divorced, raped and insane mother;

a drunken, murdering, wife-stabbing, self-shooting dead father;

having witnessed the above;

going all her life to real school and having been expelled thrice.

Tracy was deserving of compassion but from a distance. But Tracy loved the Houdinis as though she had discovered them and no fang-baring did more than excite her delighted curiosity. She studied them with the pleasure and passion of a devoted anthropologist. She remained Lilo's friend and even stayed overnight sometimes, driving Acantia to desperation.

'Lesbians! LESBIANS! Get out get out get out!'

Acantia ripped the blankets off Tracy and Lilo who were cuddled up in Lilo's bed giggling. The little naked girls stood on the wooden floor with their mouths covered and their eyes popping out of their heads at each other.

'Put some clothes on!' Acantia threw a handful of clothes from the gaping wardrobe at them and vanished out the door in a puff of smoke.

Lilo and Tracy rolled about on the floor in an agony of laughter for a few minutes before they could get dressed. Then they raced off to find the rest and tell.

Tracy was resilient. She was the only outsider who found Acantia amusing. She had no inhibitions: if something tasted horrible, she said, 'Yuk!' and refused to eat it.

Acantia said that Tracy was a sexually precocious delinquent who needed an operation, but Tracy said words were only words.

Tracy told Lilo everything there was to know about sex from a ten year old's point of view. Lilo taught Tracy how to set snares for rabbits. They never caught a rabbit, but they did take the fresh body of a snake Pa had killed by the woodpile. Lilo skinned it, cleaned it and cooked it with garlic and onions. Tracy said 'yuk' and 'poor snake', and Lilo was startled on both counts.

Tracy gave Lilo half her clothes and showed her how to use make-up. When Count Ugolini said they looked sexy, Tracy said to his face, 'In your dreams, you dirty old man.'

Lilo and Tracy fortified each other. With Ursula appearing so rarely in her life, Lilo needed weapons.

Sneaking home gave Ursula a strangely powerful feeling. The burned-out bush was fascinatingly transformed. She liked it. She wore black and streaked her cheeks with charcoal. Ember had no grave that she could find. She had fingered the truck tracks that could have been how bodies were carted away. She felt the black powdery trunks of the stringybarks as a monument to terrible freedom. She could come and go at will, catch a bus, visit her guilt and fear and dismay, and then farewell them again, and escape to Speed's arms and admiration, and the drama of telling him select bits of her story. So long as she was unseen, Ursula was like a visiting angel, sitting in judgment. But staying completely unseen was very difficult. It was almost as if Acantia could smell her, or the house itself was giving her away. For months, out of a certain superstition, she didn't enter the house at all, but would watch Acantia and her siblings from afar, spooked by the steady stare

Acantia could direct at her hiding place. She would leave, laughing, skipping into a quickening run down the road, but feeling twisted nonetheless.

Sitting on a large flaky rock, staring down at the house far below, screened by the backlit filigree of burned bushes and trunks, and with a tummy full of outside food, Ursula could see that the world of Whispers was more hurtful, more damaging than was absolutely necessary. 'Parents shouldn't do that sort of thing,' she said to herself primly. She was thinking about Lilo's laughing account of Tracy's impact on the family. She was trying not to see Acantia's point of view. She could see Whispers now for what it was, view it scientifically. Objectively. If Social Services knew about this, they'd take Siegfried, Lilo and Arno away from Acantia, they certainly would. Maybe even Helmut. And yet as she thought it, she knew that Social Services would never grasp what Siegfried, Lilo and Arno had done to Acantia and how punishment purified things and made what little love there was manifest in the world. Were she ever to pluck up the courage to speak with Social Services, she knew they would make a skewed assessment. They would not perceive evil in the victims or in Ursula herself.

As she watched, Acantia and Pa bounced and rocked up the track in the sedan, over the hill below her and away. She jumped up, and headed down to the house. It sighed as she entered. She wandered through, feeling its filth and strangeness, looking with fresh eyes at everything that was once like her second skin. It leaned in at her. 'Disgusting,' she said out loud, to stave off its familiarity and keep her objectivity. She walked through more rapidly than she had planned, out to the enclosed verandah.

Acantia had been painting.

A mean and murky red had crept into some of the paintings. It was not even, seemingly, a choice. It was the passive collusion of Acantia's frugality, prolific output and failing vision. It was the sort of thing the house would have suggested. Stale blood red. The masonites were sealed with a red that was neither cadmium red nor a mix with Vandyke brown and, instead of painting reds any more, she allowed the background to be anything red she required. This lurking red had begun to take over and the latest pictures were dominated by it. Ursula found she hated them even though some of them were good. The red seemed to be the negative of things, the opposite of painting something. Acantia was depainting. Acantia was changing too, and Ursula didn't want her to. Ursula wouldn't know whom she was fighting if Acantia changed too much.

She left in a hurry, feeling dirty and torn. Shouldn't her loyalty be to Acantia too, not just the kids?

Ursula's anger and certainties didn't last. She visited Acantia and Pa openly now and then, but stopped sneaking up to Whispers to watch her parents and hear gossip from her brothers and sister after the day she realised finally that she missed Acantia. One day Siegfried looked at her coldly when she said Acantia was cute and she felt numb inside at his disapproval. He was right. Acantia wasn't cute. Then, another day the same week when everyone was at school or out, she snuck into Acantia's bedroom. Cushioned in the strange fug of her mother's sweat and breath, she went through Acantia's drawers and cupboard. Acantia didn't have much. All her things were grimy and old or torn. Some were paint-splattered, but there was no fresh paint any more. Ursula took out a grey nightie, recognising dizzily that it was the one Acantia had worn when Arno was born. She held it to her face and smelled that old familiar abyss, and then lay down with it on Acantia's bed, something she had never done, something that, although unspoken, was utterly forbidden. She held the nightie against her chest and stared up at the ceiling Acantia saw every morning and night and through the days she didn't appear, which was often now, Siegfried had said. The bed was damp with ancient sadnesses, terrible to soak in. The ceiling dangled streamers of dusty cobwebs towards her. Acantia's room was like a cell. There was no sign in it, other than the nightie, of any of the children. It had nothing that gave any pleasure. It was the antithesis of the rooms Ursula had decorated in the Halfway House. Ursula began to weep with no warning. She turned to Acantia's greasy pillow and clenched it to her wet face. She could smell the cleanness rising from her own skin and hair. Acantia would without doubt smell that she had been here. The thought only made her cry harder. Her heart felt like a burning hole in her chest. How could she have left Acantia?

Time passed. Conditions at Whispers deteriorated. Ursula still visited occasionally, but was physically ill every time. She talked confidently to Siegfried, Helmut, Lilo and Arno about leaving home, but began to feel that she couldn't help them, didn't even want to see them, until they did. As they grew, rather than craving their company and news of their lives, Ursula found that she didn't want to hear it. She could not have said whose suffering was the greater, theirs or Acantia's, but knowing of both paralysed her.

When Helmut turned fourteen he started to smoke and smoulder. Helmut Tarsini was wrapped in a halo but the Houdinis' Helmut simply stank and glowered. Acantia called it puberty but it was obviously much more than that. He was erupting.

Helmut went out setting live chooks alight and howling like a banshee.

Siegfried joined him and Arno followed them, wide-eyed and silent.

Lilo, Siegfried and Arno gathered by the top dam, exhausted with the day's carnage, and smoked, empty and bereft. The water rippled in the summer breeze, reflecting the fire in a broken ladder of red and orange interspersed with silver from the moon. Indistinct faces stretched, broke apart and reformed endlessly in the ripples. They smoked anything they could lay their hands on. Cardboard, pine needles, basketry cane. Before long they got hold of marijuana. Lilo lit a small fire and lured Helmut in with food. He came, tucked his knees up to his chin and stared at the fire. He reached out a skinny, scarred arm, picked up a smouldering stick and used it to methodically burn the hair off his arms, legs and then his head. He didn't flinch even when his head lit up in a rush.

He looked like a match. They laughed and dowsed him with water. They all tried it on their arms but most of them flinched. Helmut had scabs for weeks.

Arno watched it all but did nothing to stop them. He stopped talking altogether for a year. He stopped sleeping. He stopped attending school. Acantia ignored his presence around the house even when he was in the same room as her until 4 pm, when she looked up and caught his eye conversationally.

'How was school?'

By unspoken agreement with his mother, Arno ceased to exist between the hours of 8 am and 4 pm. He had difficulty finding himself every afternoon at the magic hour. When he was fourteen, he suddenly started to scream and didn't stop. The hours turned into days. He screamed into the night, prowling around the outside of the house into the sodden night, screaming about Acantia and dying, petrol-drenched animals. The rain fell down in wintry shards, stinging his hot, salty face. He stared up into the black leaden sky and could bear not one second more. His voice twisted out of him inchoate, a hellish conch call.

'Don't mind Arno,' Acantia said to Lilo and Count Ugolini, who was visiting, 'He's just showing off.'

THE SUN

A harsh solar beard from the underside of the red sun slashes the chords and chasms of a still ocean. Heavy cliffs and banks of red hang in the sky, looming suspended from the darkening indigo. White haze boils from the misshapen sun. Long horizontal fingers of dead blue reach in towards the gold and white sun path, the shining crevasse closing. Cold heat. Sunset. Embers.

This was the last painting Acantia made using real paint.

Lilo walked stoned through the house and saw it magically altered. The ceiling arched high above, glimmering benignly. The walls parted and formed rooms of substantial dimensions, aglow with colour and light. The paintings became translucent and vistas of the fields and trees rushed in to greet the eager eye. The great, gold maw of the fireplace roared like a dog ridiculously pleased to see her. The timber gleamed and the glasses in the drying-up rack said *Ding! Ding!* whenever her glance touched them.

She stood looking through a painting. The colours glistened and the feathers of the trees reached out with a long, bristly caress. She touched it with her fingertips and watched the streaks and scrolls of paint come to life. The violent horizontals and elastic verticals detached themselves from the subject and floated towards her face, losing all definitions of anything other than colour. She felt the Prussian blue flow into her veins and pulse around her body.

About the time when Helmut was shaving as much of himself off as possible, Siegfried experimented with the camouflage offered by a beard and long golden locks.

He succeeded in being inscrutable. Lacking impenetrable yellow eyes he settled for impenetrable yellow hair and speaking so slowly that it was more than anybody could stand to hear him out to the end of a sentence. He managed to drop out of all interaction almost as effectively as Arno.

His facial expressions changed and he became locked within the curse of a strange muscular disorder. When he was sad, he laughed gaily; when he was happy, he grimaced. When he wished to whisper, he shouted; and when he was weeping he grinned idiotically, dry-eyed. He became so miserable that he tried to avoid contact with people altogether.

You cannot know what goats are thinking, he had once written in his goat diary.

Up around the top dam after sunset, Siegfried, Helmut, Lilo and Tracy lay around the fire. Helmut slipped off to have sex with Tracy and hoped that Lilo wouldn't mind. Lilo didn't. She saw herself as the perfect host, providing everything her guest could desire. She wondered fleetingly: when did Helmut last wash? Then she reassured herself that the smoke and the open night air would mask and dissipate his singed polecat. He was, at least, gorgeous to look at.

Acantia leapt upon Helmut, flailing a coffee table in one hand and a chair in the other. He parried with a baseball bat with, in the onlookers' eyes, admirable sangfroid. Acantia telephoned the police.

'My son is attacking me with a baseball bat!'

They said they would come at once and asked for the address.

'Oh, it's all right, I can handle it. I just thought you should know.' She hung up.

Siegfried, Helmut and Arno descended on the house like a plague of locusts at four in the afternoon. They stole and consumed silverbeet and potatoes and rice and oil. They sorted through the car glovebox, in its seat crack, under the rubber floor cover, and Pa's suit trousers, taking any coins they could find to buy bread and margarine from the little shop a mile down the road. They rattled the house with their footsteps and broke the chairs they sat in. They smashed the kitchen window when they waved their arms about. Their weight broke the beds they slept in. Their shit filled the toilet and it broke down.

The more they stole, the less Acantia gave and the more they stole.

They felled trees, lit fires and ate rabbits.

Acantia tied their feet in their lies and watched them trip.

Supine, torpid, dormant, they stared at the sky.

Acantia ignored them and went to India for her final exams for her doctorate in Ayurvedic Medicine.

Siegfried and Helmut trudged to school, making small avalanches along the creek bed, eroding the bank with their boots. The world outside flickered on their eyeballs and was noted in the diaries of their inert hearts.

The steep slopes of the bush paddock were host to secretively placed and carefully nurtured plants. Lilo planted marijuana and Siegfried planted himself. Tiny clearings, visible only to their maker, marked the mulch and earth cradle for his army of mandrakes. He dreamed of the slow shudders of his own brood, his secret pact with the forest. The stringybarks slowly thickened their scarred trunks above his nursery as he waited for something, anything that would bring him reinforcements.

Acantia dusted Siegfried like a carpet on Saturdays, beating all the week's accumulated evil out of him. Sundays were calm with restored purity, and sometimes she even cooked and fed him. Siegfried himself felt cleaner after his beatings. School was murky and threaded with currents he couldn't gauge, and he usually felt keyed up, nasty, paranoid by Friday. Acantia belted things back into their rightful places.

Over time this changed. Siegfried began attending less and less school, and spending more and more days hunting wild goats over the back hills with a bow and arrow, fortified by marijuana. Some weeks he felt himself to be quite clean and wild when the pressure built up in the lead-up to the beating. He began wearing Robinson Crusoe-like clothes made of goat skin, and still Acantia beat him.

'School!' she screamed, breathing hard. 'It's filled you with foul ideas and you stink to high heaven with them. Dirty thinking, dirty eating, dirty body. You lurch in here every day, looking like a baboon!'

Siegfried, standing straight, suddenly grabbed her arm in midstroke, and the lash of the bridle reins fell across his reeking billygoat-hide shoulders.

'I haven't been to school once, this week,' he said quietly, but with a wobble and break in his voice.

Acantia's hands fell to her sides, and she eyed him, up and down, bewildered for a moment.

'Yes,' she said thoughtfully, almost to herself. 'I can see that.' She turned and walked away, dropping the bridle to the floor, and that was the end of Siegfried's beatings and his schooling.

Whispers was more hidden and more awake than it had ever been. The bush track was accessible now by 4WD only. Pa's battered sedan made the crossing to the outside world only by experienced navigation. Ugolini parked his car on the outside and walked in these days. The house was hidden behind the army of radiata pines spawned by the row of seven, and then on and on by each other. The fire-scarred stringybarks held on, with green furred radiata kittens at their feet. The radiatas had long ago sprung in their midst, but were now black skeletons. They could not survive fire. Long grass and whisperweed covered all, as they had when the Houdinis arrived. The house creaked and cackled now, cracking joints at night, humming tunes, picking up snippets of the viola repertoire in parody and off key. It had slumped or buckled inward a little, pulled into the mountain. The damp rooms at the back were smaller than before and unused. The front was twisted slightly, so windows and doors either wouldn't open or wouldn't close. *Sweetheart*, it called Acantia. *Sweetheart, cook us some chops*. And Acantia would cook one extra, for the house, she said, but none of them laughed. It was a sombre, reduced family around the table in the dim evenings. Their chairs rattled incessantly as they ate. The floor had skewed, so the table had to have a book under one leg, and everything small slid one way only and disappeared.

Ursula visited for Mother's Day. She had avoided visiting or even calling since Christmas. Acantia forced her to stay for the night by deliberately assuming it, but still ended up sitting alone with Pa. All the children, including Ursula, melted away into the bush at dusk.

Acantia sat alone at the table, the dim light picking out a yellow halo from the loose and tousled strands of her black hair. Her children were outside in the darkness and any passing by the window could look in and observe their mother at length without her knowing it. But her eyes were hidden in dark hollows as she stared down, tracing the grain of the wood on the table with her fingers. She looked as if she was playing a silent piano. The table was almost bare. She and Pa had called, had picked over the spinach and potatoes and salad, but no children had come. Pa had slunk off to practise in Beate's house. The viola sobbed unregarded into the darkness. Siegfried had finally stopped chopping wood. He had chopped for hours, his body shaking, screaming with each downward swing, his body shining wet. Acantia had gone outside to shout at him to stop but her six foot four son had given her such a look with the axe suspended over his head that she had just smiled nastily at him and left him to it.

Through the window, as passers-by, they caught snapshots of their mother. She buried her head in her hands and her shoulders looked frail and bony but they allowed themselves no warmth.

Ursula had deserted them and their lives had filled, flowed over and burst with the weight of horrors.

If Acantia had looked out of the window, she would have seen a faint glow in the darkness above the crater of the top dam, where bow-shot rabbit, damper and omelettes were often cooked in stolen pans and stewpot. If she had crept up to watch she could have witnessed them cut Arno down from the tree from which he had tried to hang himself and she would have seen them rub his limbs and feed him as though he was a little baby curled in their arms. She would have seen Ursula, Lilo and Tracy keening and sobbing over the pot.

That night when Helmut broke into the house for supplies,

Siegfried followed him with the axe, chopped up the oak kitchen table and stacked it neatly as firewood next to the stove. Acantia burned it the next day without a word.

Arno clarified something for Ursula. She knew she would feel guilt. *Forever*, she thought to herself with wan theatricality, trying to cheer herself up. Her hour had come, but rather than feeling like a hero, she felt like a criminal, a traitor. She was dizzy with the horror of it. It would be the most terrible thing she had ever done to Acantia, or to Arno.

She had sat with them all in the firelight, under the starlight. She was the one who knew both the inside and the outside, and she could feel them all relying on her to fix Arno. Arno lay, huge and heavy, half in her lap. She hadn't realised what weight there was in skin and flesh and bones, in the mysterious ball of a head. She had rubbed him, thinking hard. All their hands were on their littlest brother, rubbing rubbing. All their thoughts were on Ursula, the only one who could get help. Arno said nothing, silent for the first time in three weeks. They knew he was listening to their murmurs by the slow seeping of tears from his closed eyes. Ursula watched them, listened to them all whisper of love unbearable, love unlimited, and the preciousness of their little brother. 'Choizus, ya fucked-up little . . . fucker,' Lilo sobbed softly.

Ursula took Arno away from Acantia. It didn't happen straightaway, but shortly after, when Ursula arrived unannounced in a strange Commodore with a psychologist and a social worker, Siegfried, Lilo and Pa shook hands with them.

When Siegfried left he went in search of Helmut, who was travelling somewhere in the north of Queensland. They met by chance hitching opposite ways along the Bruce Highway near Townsville and then jumped onto a freight train together. The train moved at a walking pace through the hot bush, then desert. Three days and Siegfried and Helmut were ill with hunger and thirst. The train inched ever on into nothingness. They jumped off into the desert and walked away from the hopeless tracks. A mob of Murri people found them and fed them for a couple of weeks and then drove them on the back of a rickety ute to the crossroads on the Stuart Highway, sick of these wide-eyed boys who spoke nonsense and ate far too much.

They rang Acantia and Pa.

'Oh my!' Acantia said. 'They are just like me when I was young! So adventurous. Brave and *unlimited*!'

When the boys arrived home, Lilo caught Acantia eyeing them. The thin faces, sunken cheeks and eyes, the lathe-like forms and the knobbly knees seemed to perplex her. They did not look like heroes.

They both left again within a week to fight for trees. They became ardent defenders of mountain ash, *eucalyptus regnans* and *eucalyptus globuli*. They collected criminal convictions like medals and applied their peacetime skills to the war effort. They camped in platforms halfway up mountain ashes and urinated on timber-workers through narrow slit windows.

When they were locked up in Pentridge on remand after the East Gippsland Forest Blockade, they appeared on national TV.

Acantia dropped everything and raced off to help. Having wrangled her way into the jail she spent several days handing out energy water to the blockaders to keep their strength up. She cured a prison warden of piles.

When they were released and returned to Whispers, Siegfried stayed only a day. It was the turning point for the twins. Siegfried's words didn't work and his army never rose behind him to shout each word in unison to the voracious loneliness he saw in his mother's eyes. His goats were dead and gone and the East Gippsland mountain ash had fallen one by one around him.

He walked out to the pine tree that had been named after him. It took him a day to chop it down and chop it up, eating away at it and screaming with each bite of the axe. Then he walked out, down to town along the Houdini escape route to Ursula's, where he lived with her and Arno for a while.

Helmut could not see things the same way. He too had spreadeagled himself on the front of a bulldozer but the trees fell anyway, making room for plantations. Longing for the only comfort he had ever known, he returned home to his mother and to the known world. Acantia became gentle and giving to Helmut, her only loving son.

Lilo left not long after Siegfried. She packed one morning, walked into the kitchen, said 'Seeya,' and walked up the raddled bush track for the last time as a child.

For long stretches Acantia and Pa were alone, as Helmut took seasonal work as a farm labourer all over the state.

Ursula had not visited since taking Arno. The children all pictured Acantia alone at Whispers and the grief they expected, the rage they imagined, began to weigh on them after Lilo too had left. They decided one weekend to visit together, as dutiful grown-up children should.

Acantia and Pa greeted their nervous children at the door of their old home. Acantia had her arms around Pa's waist, and Pa beamed at them all. Acantia giggled at their faces, and leaned into Pa's huge frame. The children were speechless.

Ursula looked on, stunned. She yearned to hug Acantia but couldn't bear to touch her. The house was completely familiar but changed too. They were no longer able to hear it or feel it the way they had before. They all breathed in that old smell. The kitchen had a brand-new unscratched table with an unfamiliar vase of flowers in the middle. There was a tiny television on the bench (Ursula guessed without asking that a small one was less harmful than a large one).

Acantia sniffed deeply at Arno's neck as she hugged him. They all knew she was smelling for the drugs but were disoriented when she stroked his cheek and said nothing. Acantia and Pa made them lunch. Acantia twittered happily about the garden she and Pa had planted together, and how they had repainted her room. Acantia asked them about their studies and murmured approvingly, supportively about everything they had to say. 'Do you need anything?' she asked once. 'Pa and I could help out.' Something glittered behind her eyes when she looked at Ursula.

They didn't stay long. They hovered nervously, chewed mechanically, and then fled. They drove along the bush track to the highway in silence. Then, catching each other's sideways glances, they started to laugh and couldn't stop. 'Who the fuck was that!' Lilo sighed, holding her stomach, and that set them all off again. What more could anyone say?

Ursula sank more and more deeply into blank depression. She was twenty-one, an adult. Arno no longer needed her much and was back at school, attending a city school paid for in secret by Pa. He still saw the psychologist, but refused to talk to her about it. He avoided her—slowly, quietly finding himself and his independence from them all. Lilo lived in a squat with her band and visited occasionally. The Halfway House was empty from 8.30 until 4.30, unbearable, but Ursula did nothing about it. She dragged herself like a revenant to some Honours classes and home again. The Halfway House turned into something to echo Whispers for a while.

When Ursula, dry-eyed in Siegfried's salty rented flat, told him, finally, about Ugolini, Siegfried turned away and stared at the toaster. It was too much. He couldn't look closely at Ursula again. Whenever they met, Siegfried heard seagulls and stared at Ursula's hair, at her elbows, knees and fingertips and wondered about the length of her toenails inside her sneakers.

Siegfried gradually stopped seeking out his brothers and sisters altogether, but did write to them now and then, and ran into them on rare visits to Whispers. Even when he married, many years later, he invited only Acantia and Pa.

Until the fire.

dirige dominus deus meus

(many years later)

The fire was a long time coming but when it did, twenty-five years after they moved in, it was utterly effective. The house was never rebuilt.

After the fire Pa and Acantia lived in what had been Beate's house. They kept cottage alone, the lovely old childless couple in the forest. With all the children gone, Pa became the woodman. He chopped wood for the fires in the morning and tuned instruments in front of the open fire in the evenings. Acantia's hair was grey, some strands even white. Pa sometimes combed her hair, aligning the white strands harmoniously with the grey, pulling out all the black ones. She painted and mixed energy waters next to him. They were quietly in love.

Ursula, Siegfried, Lilo and Arno came home to visit more often after the fire (usually in pairs).

Pa said, *you have to focus on the positive*. In this he agreed with Acantia. *We are all in this together. We can only stay attuned to one another through effort.* His grown-up children laughed. They were cynical. They had no intention of allowing themselves to be touched or of trying to stay attuned. They muttered and growled.

'Pa sees no evil, hears no evil, speaks no evil.'

'Ha!'

'He can't even tune the piano.'

After the house burned down, Count Ugolini had sent Acantia and Pa a present of a small grand piano. His noble impracticality impressed them. Pa built a small grand piano room in one of the old burned-out dressing-rooms. The grand piano room had galvanised iron cladding made from the old sheets from the roof. Apart from enduring extremes of heat and cold, the piano had to be moved out into the open air to be played. It was never in tune.

No one really knew why Acantia stopped liking the Count. One month he was there in the auditorium looking old and gone in the tooth, talking about his illness and the false accusations trumped up against him and the corruption of the vice squad.

'Whispers is my sanctuary, my last refuge.'

The next month her face closed down at the mention of his name and she wandered about dim and ashen. She rewrote her will. She refused to consider Gotthilf.

'Gotthilf has been heartless and greedy since he was breastfeeding. I would do his soul irreparable damage if I were to help him.'

They were only mildly curious about the Count's fall from grace. It made them laugh that, right when he thought he needed Acantia, she had spurned him. They didn't take anything seriously.

'Count Ugolini was always a weak man.' Acantia shook her head slowly, staring at her porridge. 'We gave him everything that poor people could give the very wealthy. You know, nonmaterial things. The warmth of a hearth in the heart of a loving family. He has succumbed to the evil that surrounds him, I'm afraid. I could have saved him if he had had the strength to listen to me.' Acantia had made a few mistakes. She admitted them. One was to have told the Count that he was wrong to buy the biggest arms factory in the world and that he should be using his immeasurable wealth, now that his evil old father had died and left all of it to him, for the good of mankind.

'He has turned on us. Children, we are in grave danger. He is connected with the Mafiosi, oh, from way back, you know.' She looked up at her irritated brood, her face calm and serene, noble in the face of such peril. 'I could heal him from his physical afflictions, easily. But proximity to his psychic evil could only contaminate me, and then I would be no use to any of you.' She sighed heavily, and then gazed lovingly at the young men and women shuffling aggressively in front of her. How much she gave for them, her look said. Ursula snorted but changed it into a sneeze. Arno stared at the ceiling.

The Count told Acantia somewhat vengefully that the piano was hot. He had sold it to two different people before hiding it at Whispers.

Acantia was a receiver of stolen property. Should she risk their lives and the lives of all her children by telling the police the whereabouts of Lady Deadlock's historic grand piano? Ugolini had become taller, darker and more distinctly Sicilian.

Perhaps she could pass the piano on to one of her scattered six (seven) children. No good. Ugolini was multinationally tentacular.

Perhaps the police would understand if she explained everything to them. No good. The police had failed to uphold the law on many occasions. No knowing what depths of Police Corruption they might by now have plumbed.

Pa wanted to burn the piano and bury it. Everyone had some advice to offer. Ursula said to bump Ugolini off first. Acantia suggested that those who suffer from such severe imaginitis that they cannot take a family emergency seriously should keep their smart comments to themselves.

Helmut told Ursula that Ugolini was ringing up often and that Acantia was genuinely scared of him.

Immediately after the fire, Acantia was too groggy to stop them and the children had leapt upon the house like starving dogs shredding an injured pack member. They smashed down the ruined walls with battering rams. They had no thought for their own safety. Helmut stood like a fiend on the battlements smashing rubble out of the wall he was standing on with a sledgehammer. Pa and Ursula battered bricks down one by one and shook the fatigued concrete lintels free. They had lowered the ruins considerably by the time Acantia made up her mind. Then they were forbidden from battering any more.

They prowled around longing to get their teeth into it but didn't dare do more than furtive weakening of cracks.

Lilo and Ursula sat in the long summer grass at the top of the neglected orchard, staring down at the hole filled with blackened tin and rubble that had been the house. Ursula was pale under a mask of ash. 'Just the house, luckily,' the Emergency Fire Service man said, shuddering involuntarily and holding out the rescued cat. But at the heart of this fire was another, and buckled flesh and animals screamed at the back of Ursula's mind. The smell of baked apples hung heavily in the air, and even from so far away the ground and the leaves of the trees were dusted with ash. Ursula stroked a leaf, half expecting it to be greasy. It was powder. They could see Siegfried and Arno, small blackened figures, trailing their way up through the blackberry to join them. It had been a hard day. They stared at the evening sky, streaked with flames of red and gold and aqua and purple.

'Funny if the Count really does kill Pa and Acantia.'

'Shhhh,' Lilo whispered, looking sober. 'The house really *did* burn down. Bullshit comes true.'

They had all prayed for an incendiary bomb to hit the house. It had become a game, this insulting the house.

'Best thing for it would be a match and some petrol.'

'Only way to clean it up is to burn it down.'

'Pity Ash Wednesday fizzled out when faced with the Houdini House.'

'Wonder what it said.'

'Ha ha!'

There were twelve volumes of the Houdini press clippings scrap-books. HOUDINIS ESCAPE HORROR FIRE TRAP was preserved, with the other clippings that were not about Pa or Beate, in number twelve.

It was dated 16 February 1983, Ash Wednesday. Everyone knew Ursula left and then the fires started. Acantia even said that Ursula was the arsonist.

Lilo, nine years old, stood with the neighbours, her siblings and Acantia on the hill. Fire raged in the scrubland on the hill above. Smoke and ash swirled in apocalyptic rhythms and the sun was dimmed to an angry yellow. The people huddled, praying for the safety of their deserted homes left to the mercy of fate. The Houdinis' house sat below, smoking a little. Falling leaves rimmed with fire sailed gaily through the air to land on its roof. Lilo broke free from Acantia and ran to a vantage point. Her pale hair was backlit in the weird light like a halo of an avenging sprite. She began jumping up and down shaking her fists at the distant house.

'Burn! Burn! Burn! Burn! Burn!'

The neighbours looked uncomfortable.

The house had burned down exactly fifteen years and a day later. One by one, they gathered on the same hill to stare down at the twisted asbestos-powdered wreckage below, half laughing and half scared that they had all once wished for this. Ursula and Lilo rocked together, almost crying.

The two sisters sat through the wild sunset with their arms about each other's necks, breathing the darkening summer in and out.

In adulthood, Ursula and Lilo became friends. It wasn't clear to Ursula why Lilo would like her, only that Lilo always had, with passionate, blind partiality. For her part, Ursula admired Lilo without envy. She admired Lilo's beauty, her fearlessness, and held her close as carefully as one might cuddle a bomb.

It was amusing, if foolhardy, to humiliate Lilo.

Ursula had once picked her tiny sister up, folded her in half in a bear hug and thrown her out the door. The door crashed back open as if struck by lightning. Lilo stood there looking like a fiend. Her blonde curls stood out around her face and her eyes were torches. Ursula started to laugh. Lilo leapt in one bound to the dish-rack and grabbed the breadknife. Then she lunged with all her might at Ursula, screaming, 'I am going to POP YOU!'

Later she said that she wanted to prick all of them like balloons; change their laughing faces. Give them extra holes.

Helmut had to hold her down, sit on her scuttling, sea-crab body and wrench the knife off her while she pinched and bit him. Ursula was laughing helplessly, even though she knew that Lilo meant it, and that she was in greater danger then than from any dust-up with Acantia.

As young women, Lilo was outrageous where Ursula was shy and complicated. Lilo tried everything. Ursula preferred to read or hear about it. Lilo once said to Ursula, 'Stop analysing, or I'll belt ya.'

Lilo refined rage to an art form. She stopped playing classical violin when she was fourteen and began improvising. Pa stopped teaching her in disgust. And from then on she was alone with her instrument. She stopped holding the bow as she had been taught and stopped using major, minor or chromatic scales in any properly recognisable form, and she messed with all forms of cadence or transition. Her music became irreverent. Not long after leaving

Whispers, she fitted a pick-up to her instrument and painted purple and red screaming mouths, glaring eyes and vampire teeth all over it. A snake wound around the neck. She became well known as a busker in Melbourne and was increasingly in demand for alternative no-budget film tracks. She began playing for a punk folk band. Her violin screeched and howled, torturing listeners, then shocking them with exquisite songs. Pa asked Ursula to ask Lilo to change her name. Lilo refused.

Deep in the belly of the Goat and Compasses, punk folk rage pumped out into the anaesthetised and appreciative audience. Lilo's voice was the thread of the lonely violin glowing like an ember in the damp grey smoke of urban student rebellion. But the anarchists of the Goat and Compasses were a little shaken by Lilo and her band ditched her for a more uniform sound and the name Plastiscene.

Lilo attended their inaugural gig as the malevolent fairy.

She gave them the gift of her invective.

'Yas *SUCK*! Don't give up ya fucken *DAY JOBS*!'

She gave them the gift of minor missiles.

'Have a *BEER*!'

She gave them an electric shock and the bouncers threw her out.

She burst down the door in an adrenaline rush, carrying the stone trough full of dogs' water, drenched the stage and crushed the amp. She was banned from the Goat and Compasses for life. She sat on the pub windowsill like an enraged black cat for a couple of weeks but was spooking too many people and was banned from that as well.

Lilo grinned at Ursula and raised her eyebrows, golden eyes alight.

'You have to do quite a bit to get banned for life from an anarchists' club!'

Three months after the fire, Lilo took off overseas on a one-way ticket, planning to busk her way around the world. Ursula got several cards from Budapest and felt deserted.

One day, a month or so before the first Christmas after the fire, Ursula was evading her thesis in the university library, browsing in recently acquired journals. She thumbed idly through a copy of the new literatures journal, *Rage*; then her short hair rose straight in the air all over her scalp. One of the contributors had her name. *Ursula Houdini*. There it was in the index. There in the volume: *Ursula Houdini*. There, in the list of contributors: *Ursula Houdini is an Australian writer of fiction and other untruths*. She knew immediately that it was Gotthilf. He had maintained contact at a cryptic trickle until two years before and then severed it altogether when he heard that Acantia had spoken about getting custody of his daughter. No one had his current address.

Ursula had written rarely and had not seen him since he ran away.

'THREE LIES A NOVELIST MAKE'

BY URSULA HOUDINI

Her eyes blurred and her mind buzzed with white noise. *A novelist!* It was a silly piece about truth, fantasy and lies, and the role of parents in helping children understand the difference. She skimmed it, heart pounding. Then, suddenly, it was about her and him, and she was snagged and pulled under into his terrible joke.

> *. . . There can be a devil-may-care desperado glamour to the great child liar. For myself, however, I lacked the charisma to make a vocation of lying. I struggled to regain the mainstream, someone who might be believed one day, who might be certified as having the Truth, the Lies and the Fantasies firmly defined and even a weapon which, by virtue of my seniority and good name, I could impose on others. I was more craven than my older brother,* il miglior fabbro. *After three great lies he accepted that his state was irredeemable, scoffed at shame and guilt and launched a blazing career. My brother was the audacious bushranger of mendacity, the reprobate, and every word he uttered was hunted down and put on trial. He made raids on the truth, spicing his lies with just enough to make works of art of them. He made lying beautiful and brave; he lied for the aesthetics of it, not just for self-interest. He became the Anti-Truth, the great threat to the world of reason. He became powerful in his own way, shaking the foundations of everything my parents stood for: reason, science and a consensus on what is real and what is not. He was king of a space they couldn't enter, unless they were prepared to lie too. He led a charmed life, replacing trust and veracity with stories giving off a golden glow, until disaster struck.*

All of us children (there were seven kids in our family) wanted to be heroes, warriors, martyrs. We dreamed of being the one to rescue hapless folk from burning houses. We were each convinced, or at least hopeful, of our staunch, unflinching bravery in the face of danger. We would, given the opportunity, catch snakes by the neck with our lightning reflexes. We would stand and calmly hand the frightened people a place in the lifeboat and, dry-eyed, go down with the ship. Silent on the rack, on the gallows, the guillotine, the executioner's block. Bystanders would remark on our pale, calm faces as we died, innocent of any crime, doing far far better things. We led the charge of the Light Brigade. We were the underground Resistance. We longed for opportunity to prove it.

My brother went to New Zealand for a holiday. He was swimming nonchalantly in the shallows when he saw a mother and child screaming and coursing steadily on the current out to sea. Adrenaline rushing through him, he scampered over the rocks to the last bastion before the open sea . . . well the long and short of it was that he, with utmost bravery and disregard for himself, saved both their lives. There were no witnesses and he forgot to get their names in writing, so elated was he with the serendipitous transition he had just made from Anti-Truth to Hero.

I think the bitterest day of his life was the day he came home. Chest swelling, words falling out of mouth, he, with an uncharacteristic lack of cool, poured out the story to his mother and father.

Once you are an established liar, you generally know the difference between lies and truth. While you are in the early experimental stages, everything you say might or might not be true, you tell yourself. Once you are cast out from the garden with public exposure and ignominy, you tend to accept that it was the latter. You begin to fantasise about what it would be like to be believed, even if you were lying.

Three great lies do make a liar of you. Telling the truth slowly becomes redundant. You have no choice but to grow up, burdened by the weight of lies, real and perceived, and then become a novelist in order to begin fabricating the great truths your lies have unearthed.

Ursula sat stunned for a moment, boiling and cold.

In it he stole more than her name, but it was about him, and it was, she thought, written for her eyes only. Only she, Ursula, could have picked the half-truths and the lies. He had to have known that she was an English postgrad, had to have hoped she would stumble across it.

The cheek of it! But with her rising anger there rose in her something else altogether. The delight that he would take the energy to poke and prod her! To think that he thought of her, even knew and remembered so much. She found herself weeping, humbled. She began to sob, and smile, hugging her brother to her chest.

She thought of Gotthilf and Ursula in the abstract, looking on. How much they knew of each other! What secrets they shared. What terrible partners their bodies were. Her mind slid, in the abstract, to the reason she had shut Gotthilf out. She thought of Ugolini and *that*, coldly. She wondered how she could have let her brother go, when he had so endearingly, cheekily, been able to keep a hold on her.

How dare he! The monster. She laughed out loud. She was shaking.

She stole the copy of the journal.

The next day she was at the library at opening time and searched the Austlit database for 'Houdini'. She found one entry. He had published a story in an anthology entitled *Women on Men*. She ordered it on interlibrary loan, torn now with a twisted longing and grief over the past. She kept laughing through tears at him, with him. He had really got them a good one.

The book took two weeks to arrive. In that time Ursula stopped all research, all preparation for Christmas. She scoured databases and bookshops. If he had a book, he had buried it far more cunningly than the article and the story. At first she thought that it had to be offshore; then, because her name threw up nothing, she became convinced that there was no book. Then she woke up one morning knowing with sudden clarity that there was, and that it was not published under anything as easy as their names. She searched through all the telephone directories in Australia for both his name and her own, but found nothing. She imagined storming in on him somewhere, waving his stories, calling him to account, and seeing him grin, cheekily. And the thought of having him there in front of her, delighted at the success of his scheme, filled her with a shuddering terror that she couldn't define. She telephoned and asked Pa for any information on Gotthilf's latest address. Pa was silent for a moment. Then, his voice annoyed, he said, 'We don't want any encyclopaedias, thank you,' and hung up on her. She asked all her brothers and sisters. No one knew. Gotthilf had disappeared.

Then 'Topend' arrived over the interlibrary loans desk. There was no bio, no further clue. Just the story.

'TOPEND'
by URSULA HOUDINI

Helmut Houdini cycled from Port Augusta to Darwin in midsummer on an old Bullock pushie with a goatskull bolted to the steering column for handlebars, ten litres of water in panniers, a hat and a homemade swag.

He was not an ordinary young man.

For one thing he was very beautiful. His sisters called him Rufus, partly because he was lean and hard and golden-red and partly because it rhymed with Dufus. Helmut had copper-gold dreadlocks, standing out about his head like a fiery halo. He looked like a prophet, saint or devil but he had the eyes of a celestial puppy. They were deep set, of a bluewater ocean colour. They usually shone with an interplay of hungers, the strongest of which was the desire for human company.

Helmut perches with unconscious grace, staring intensely at the men seated next to him along the bar of the Burke and Wills, picking up their discarded words like souvenirs or treasure.

'My oath. Them Inderneejuns f'sure.'

'Yep. Guns, ammo, nukular warheads—just two hundred miles thataway.' The big, miserable looking man points with the flicker of an eyebrow. 'And they's Muslims.' Everyone mutters.

'Yup. More ammo than the whole Australian army.'

The fan sighs above them, its blades starting no planes. A gecko is upside down on one of them.

Helmut hears the same rumbles and grumbles wherever he goes. Darwin is squashed between the thumb and forefinger of the sky and earth. The build-up has brought the air to the boil early and has simmered it for months until the fine rich soup burns the nasal passages and brains with its heady and intolerable spices.

'Darwin'll get it first. You'll see. Like in '42. Boom, out of the blue. Fires and bits of ships all over the town. An airborne croc bought down a plane.'

The men hmmm hmmm hmmm yeah into their beers. Helmut pretends he too has heard it all before but his eyes leap about uncontrollably.

Mutter Mutter

Darwin is seething and rumbling with fear-mongering and bitterness, deserted by the army and the navy to suffer its stewpot summer alone. The Fanny Bay cannons are stuffed with tissues, nappies, needles and condoms. One good shot at the invaders with that lot should do the trick. No one even laughs.

Mutter Mutter

Helmut doesn't take it too seriously—he is a visiting nutter, not a beetle pinned to the earth. Darwin sweats greenness and he has never seen anything like it. For a rufus red-desert man, who drank his way overland in ten litre gulps, it is soothing to the eyeballs and the words of humankind are like water.

The first mortar struck with no warning.

It had been a strange day. The air was expectant, as if prescient.

Lurid streaks stained an aqua-green sky above violet clouds. Nothing moved. The sea was grey glass, brittle and silent. Helmut spent the day fitting a headlight into his goatskull. He had just dossed down in the bush on the outskirts of the city when the nightsky was split in half by a channel of incandescent flame. The noise filled every orifice of his body, followed by the tingling suction of an awful silence. Then the blitz began in earnest. Darwin was being bombed to oblivion and the sky was shot through with strafing tracers, searchlights, flak and the screaming descent and impact of mortars.

Helmut was galvanised into action.

Legs pumping with adrenaline, he pedals madly south down the velvet-black Stuart Highway. He imagines the lovely green city behind him, the fires, the fish and ships smashed to bits in the harbour. Tears run down his face, lit up in the odd afterglow of his dim eyesocket headlights. A few raindrops the size of conkers fall from the sky.

He pushes through the night, knowing that he is pedalling on the rim of Australian history. The invaded city looms darkly in his mind, smouldering as the bombing ceases and the gunfire begins. He holds onto his strings of words, gingerly. Perhaps he is carrying their last words on earth. He pedals. A car passes, piled up with all the worldly goods a family could throw together. Faces stare back, reflecting his own shocked excitement and terror, as they pull rapidly out of the glow of his skull lights and disappear south. He pedals, eating up the kilometres of the dark highway. The tumult dies and the machine-gun rattle becomes faint and intermittent. The road glows ahead like a pale knifeblade. He pedals, homesick suddenly for the burned gold and red summer at the edge of the southern blue sea.

Two hundred kilometres from Darwin, Helmut stops with the dawn, awed and exhausted, sombre as Anzac Day. In the Chicken Lickin' Roadhouse the people look stunned, shocked bloodless, stoic. He leans, wide-eyed, towards a truckie who is chatting to the girl behind the doughnuts and Snickers bars.

'Pretty bad about the war, aye.'

The truckie stares the golden boy up and down, nods vaguely and moves slightly away, turning back to the girl behind the Snickers.

'A real topender, last night. Right above Darwin. Bloody beautiful, if ya ask me.'

Ursula crumbled. She left the bookshops and the library and went home to curl up and think about Gotthilf. She had to see him, but couldn't move. What had happened, really, all those years ago? She, Ursula, had written nothing. Where did Gotthilf find the energy to goad, tease and love an idea of his brothers and sisters? How did he know? How did he manage to care? This absent and dismissed boy who had watched, crowed and written about them.

She stayed day after day on greying sheets, unwashed and staring.

Lilo suddenly appeared at her front door the week before Christmas, told Ursula she stank, and made her get up and have a shower. Lilo was bright-eyed, secretive, knowing. Waiting. Uninformative about her time in Budapest.

'Bin writing lately?' she said, suddenly, grinning.

Lilo had found another story in an American science fiction e-zine. Ursula felt as though she had been expecting this. Waiting for it.

'They are Gotthilf,' Ursula whispered.

It was a story that entered deeply into Arno's world.

'OUTER SPACE'

By URSULA HOUDINI

Arno's computer crashed.

For perhaps three months he had sat with its gentle blue glow illuminating his face, shining through his ears and its sweet hum ringing on into his sleep and dreams. Occasionally he had wandered out into the sunlight, blinking, surprised at the rapidity of the transition from spring to summer and so on. The dog shit on the bottom step of the crumbling stair, which had been brown, was now white and brittle-looking. It was refreshing. He would sit for ten minutes on his rotted sloping verandah, imagining a stream of molecules bombarding his skin. He could almost see vitamin D. Soon, however, he would imagine that he could see UV smashing the D, destroying the forces of benevolent molecular health, and, vanquished, he would turn in, back to the gentle blue.

He curled up on his mattress and tried to keep his eyes shut. After two weeks of absolute despair in which he could only find the milky glow in troubling dreams, he found himself staring up at the black screen on the desk in the corner. He didn't know the town. He had only ever been to the deli and the Centrelink. When there were grapes on the vine or plums on the plum tree, he didn't go out for a fortnight at a time. Faced with the blank screen, he could see himself already, computer in his backpack, descending the winding footpath into the city for help. He shut his eyes again.

He had a bad feeling as he unplugged the modem, the power supply and the printer and packed the computer into its special carry case. His world, his spaceship, packed into a small square of plastic then stashed on his back. He turned to face the world outside.

Just out the door and everything was going well. He shared his street with several slowly composting old weatherboard houses and, twenty steps past them, a glass-fronted Centrelink and a Past-The-Use-By-Date, his favourite sort of deli. He was at the top of the street and beginning the descent down the gorge-side footpath before he knew it. The gorge stretched to his right, looking wild and glorious. The distant water looked like a sheet of silver, a glittering screen of no colour. The sky was that refracted glaring white which is neither clouds nor clear. He knew a bit about weather and noticed things with quiet satisfaction. The path descended sharply into trees, ferns and mossy rocks, and a general profusion of the spill-over from gardens run wild down the cliff side. The water was a long way down and soon vanished, glimmering only now and then through the thick greenery.

He knew the map of the city pretty much off by heart. He made a point of knowing exactly where he was and had bookmarked the map of the CBD months before. He knew that at the bottom of the gorge path there would be a bridge and he would have to turn right. He was not completely sure where he would find a computer service centre but had a fair idea, from his knowledge of the layout of cities and business districts, where, according to maximum need density, there should be one.

The descent was much longer than he had anticipated. His initial triumph at finding the path gave way to a sense of unease and his body heated up. He was almost sure the path could not have been this long. A picture he had used as a screensaver in grape season leapt into his mind. Inspired by it, he had learned quite a lot about Japanese painting. It was of a wild and rocky mountain painted in black and red ink, bigger than the frame of the screen. A Japanese mountain that could have extended indefinitely up and down. In the centre there was a figure, bent over a staff, carrying an aged parent down a craggy and treacherous mountain path.

He cheered up and forgot the screensaver when he came upon a cherry-plum tree laden with fruit. The ground under it was spattered with the flesh and blood of fallen fruit and the strange yellow skulls of pips. He had had no idea that it was plum season. In fact he was sure that it wasn't. Some trick of the gorge-side shelter and the water and light catchment. He picked one cautiously and popped it into his mouth. It was full and tight, sweet, tart and juicy. He had never had one like it. He stood and ate several kilos of fruit, spitting the pips this way and that. His hope rose, although he could smell a strange smell.

A little further down the path, he saw something. He cut short his soft whistling and held his breath. Something had moved. Just then a life form he had never seen darted into the pathway and smashed a bottle at his feet. It was gone again in a second, screaming in abusive tones something that sounded like 'Christmas cake!' but could not have been. He had not really seen much but had a vague impression of a biped mammalian type, a little bandicootish. He was very shaken and stared around fearfully. He wanted to go home but the pressure of the increasingly heavy black case against his back pushed him on. He felt an ugly anxiety pick up his heart and toss it back and forth. The smell was stronger.

The first time you see an alien life form in the flesh is one of those dizzying moments which is followed by considerable self doubt and the resurgence of other often more plausible fears. Arno hurried down the steps, driven by images of aliens and cyborgs which he had enjoyed on-screen, comfortable then, even admiring. He became worried about inner space, outer space and cyberspace. He'd read Sean Williams' latest. He knew quite a bit about aliens and speculative worlds, was impressed by them because they were imaginary. He felt ill.

He tried to tell himself that it was someone in fancy-dress who had indeed said something loudly about Christmas cake.

He came upon a sign that said City, and above it another word in marks he could just recognise as a font of some kind. He hurried past it. His mind couldn't work smoothly. He shook as if he had a virus. Something had happened. His skin was so pale! His hair was so long! Something had happened in time and space. His backpack pressed into his damp back. Why wasn't it on the news? He had scrolled through the news religiously every morning. Always the same server.

What if he had been watching the wrong news?

He suddenly found himself at the bottom of the gorge-side path. To his right was a wide bridge spanning the river. Sweating, he went over to the parapet and looked down. He was almost unsurprised. The water was a translucent yellow.

He could still smell something.

He started down the street, noticing everything. The pathway was cobbled with a springy green material he didn't recognise. His heart still lurched sickeningly but Arno wasn't stupid. Life was obviously happening all around him pretty smoothly. He would keep to himself, make a beeline for the CBD, hope his estimations were correct, get the computer fixed, race home and sit down and find out exactly what had happened. He crossed the bridge with his head down, only just registering that he had two shadows.

Something was really not right but he would think about it later. He had to start looking up to avoid bumping into aliens.

There were no humans on the crowded streets. Everyone stared. It was like the first day at a new school. Arno blushed deeply and twined his fingers in his backpack straps. A young female biped with wild hair above an indescribable face strode towards him, towing an extraordinarily ugly quadruped. She brushed Arno and whispered in oddly accented English into his ear as she passed, 'Seeya later.' Arno turned to look at her lithe form just as the quadruped looked back and stuck its tongue out at him.

By the time he reached what he supposed was the CBD, furtive glances had allowed him to begin classifying the creatures around him by type. Unless they used English, which was rare, he could not catch even the sound threads of their language; but it was clear that there were many more bipeds than quadrupeds and that the latter were perhaps enslaved. There were equine, ovine, even elephantine types among the bipeds. He almost laughed to himself at the paucity of his own imagination: he had to fall back on the known in order to observe the strange world he had found himself in. He was not exactly enjoying himself but he did feel that tingling rush one feels upon discovering a new and splendid website hidden on some remote server in Greenland.

He was finding the scrutiny of strange creatures acutely embarrassing.

Deep in the CBD, buildings towered over him, glinting red and yellow lights from stacks of faceless reflective windows. Shops lined the street in an oddly familiar fashion. Perhaps commerce forms the same arrangement anywhere, Arno thought sagely. He didn't recognise most of the shops. He couldn't read most signs and the displays were more often than not unfamiliar. He found a computer retailer easily enough, however, relief washing through him as he recognised from some distance the gentle call and the soft glow. Praying to himself that retailers also serviced, he entered shyly and the shop fell silent except for the mellifluous hum of whirring drives and screens. Six bipeds stared at him. Flushed and fumbling in an agony of embarrassment, Arno slipped his backpack off, slid the case out, clicked the catch open with sweating thumbs and lifted his sad square of plastic onto a counter behind which a hirsute and swarthy creature, a porcine, was waiting. An awful silence ensued. Eyes to the floor, Arno whispered the word 'Crash'. The creature inclined its head suddenly and took the computer, disappearing behind a silver wall. The other creatures began whispering, eyeing Arno now and then. In the still air of the shop, he realised with surprise that the smell was him. He sniffed his bare arm. Arno began to have a very bad feeling, surrounded here by whispers he couldn't quite hear, by a smell that was him, and by blue glows and hums none of which would ever be his. He felt suddenly bereft.

The bristling porcine type had returned. It snorted, not unkindly, 'Motherboard's fucked.'

Arno stared down at his sunburned arms. He had four shadows, forming a faint X marking the spot on which he stood.

He knew that he would never be going home.

Lilo read the other two, giggling while Ursula sobbed and whimpered as though unmasked.

Lilo sighed blissfully. 'Choizus! 'Now, THAT is a Christmas joke.' She turned on Ursula, eyes glinting. 'Why you? Hmmm? Why's he got it in for you?'

Ursula didn't answer. There were some things she had never told Lilo, and she was suddenly glad. Yes she had told Lilo about herself. But in this one thing she had been loyal to Gotthilf. She had told no one, not even Lilo, not even when she and Gotthilf had seemingly drifted out of each other's lives.

But the last lines stung and rang on with her all afternoon. Arno's obsession with computers was well known. The rest of it was about all of them, Acantia buried so deep that she would never recognise herself. The last lines were a message. She went quiet, reached for the papers and reread all three pieces for other messages, but there was nothing that stood out beyond the obvious.

Later that night, alone in crisp clean sheets folded over her mattress for her by Lilo, she thought more calmly, more brutally over it all.

What had really happened to her and Gotthilf that made him pick her, blame her for his airy, laughing genius? They had fucked the same slick old predator, or rather been fucked by him. She had curled up while her brother had flourished, pinching her name. She was jealous. She was relieved. She was delighted, flattered, hurt, heartbroken. But above all, accused. There was so much love in his treachery, and so much betrayal in her loyalty.

How could *she*, of all of them, have forgotten Gotthilf?

Ugolini had made her feel the seductress, made her think she was the one who chose. *You are so beautiful that you are like the idea of purity. Your body can be given, a great gift, ennobling you in the giving. Would you give it to me?* And after. After. She hadn't fully grasped that he really meant sex while he undressed her. She had thought during the nightmare that sex was the initiation, not the end. When he fell asleep he looked like a dead body. He had strange blotches on his bare skin, and his open mouth was pallid. She waited for something beyond the vague terror of being alone after sex with Acantia due home soon. Nothing came, only sobs.

Gotthilf's face the day she realised. She had not warned him when he was sent away to stay with Ugolini. She remembered being jealous, feeling discarded.

It was disgust that had kept her unloving. Disgust at innocence. At being duped. At knowing that her secret was shared. Disgust that it was just swindle and appetite and the way of the world.

But she never knew that Gotthilf had known. And she couldn't bear it.

She had not once called Acantia to account for Gotthilf. She had not once really questioned the beatings that kept his skin broken and the bruises on his ribs. Perhaps she had wanted him beaten. She had done nothing because there was nothing beautiful or noble about Ursula if snivelling, scrawny, flinching Gotthilf got fucked too.

She needed his book, sure now of what it would contain. Hoping that it forgave her. She got up at midnight, turned on the computer and began to write it.

It had taken nearly a decade and the fire for Siegfried to resurface. He emerged as someone who took no shit from Acantia and saw his brothers and sisters in controlled environments. Acantia called him a lazy good-for-nothing in vain. Siegfried simply said No, capriciously and without explanation, to everything; but didn't stop phoning her and Pa.

'Siegfried, will you and Isa be coming over for Christmas?'

'No.'

But he still came.

He arrived first with his wife and baby. It was a warm December afternoon. Whispers was beautiful. Redolent. Ghost-riddled. Pain-riven.

Lilo arrived in an F100 pick-up. She had been away for eighteen months and Acantia, Pa and Helmut had not seen her since she'd got back. She had wintered in a squat in Budapest, burning furniture for warmth and playing street violin, before returning to Melbourne to work as a freelance prostitutes' bodyguard. She had become an urban commando, fighting skinheads and anyone else who annoyed her. She was lean and mean, pierced and gap-toothed. She had tattoos. A rat rode on her shoulder. To compensate for her indestructible beauty, she carried weapons upon her person. No one asked why she came to Christmas fully armed.

Acantia told her to wash the dishes but hugged her tight.

Acantia was very sweet to Toxique the rat.

Pa said, 'Prettypolly, arrrrr, me hearty,' and they all laughed.

Arno arrived, smiling shyly, with Lilo. He had long golden hair, a small red beard and moustache, and a laptop. He lived on sickness benefits, but had saved for the computer by restricting his diet to soya beans, lentils, margarine, onions, eggs and spinach for ten months.

Beate arrived in a taxi with alien-looking luggage and wearing make-up. They were all shocked at how little she was—no taller than Acantia. Beate had an accent. Beate walked straight out of family legends into life again. She had left her children in safety in the other hemisphere. She tried to cover her horror at being home for Christmas under a brittle shell of breathless excitement. She could not hide her shock at the burned-out ruin.

She ran around ringing the bells of memory until Lilo said, 'Bring out your dead.'

Beate laughed hysterically and then began to cry.

Ursula arrived on foot. Speed dropped her at the bottom of the track—after all these years she still didn't bring Speed to Whispers. She looked around for Gotthilf, hoping wildly, but she could see from everyone's manner that Gotthilf's return could not be. She had the sudden thought that it would fix everything as suddenly as the fire—but then, how could anything be fixed?

Gotthilf didn't come home for Christmas.

Acantia and Pa had created a spectacular edifice out of the burned-out ruins.

Acantia stood with her arms held wide. Her face was crinkled up into its yearning, loving look and Ursula felt herself slewing sideways, sinking towards old selves. Acantia was very small, dressed in something that was still white. She rushed around her tall children, eager to touch them, eager to show everything she and Pa had done, eager for their approval and armed to the teeth against any criticism.

She had rebuilt most of what they had ripped down. She had built beautiful, even flourishing, gardens throughout the ruins. She had packed the floor with compressed dolomite. It was an inside-out house. The enclosed verandah was roofed and windowed but the rest was nearly all open to the sky. A Japanese-style bridge made out of slabs of polished river redgum joined the remains of the auditorium to the outer garden.

Ursula roamed through it all in the elated, exhausted dream-world of a woman who has been writing all night. Replete and empty, seeking more. She felt as though she was undersea diving, seeing her family for the first time. How would Gotthilf feel, seeing it all after such cataclysm, such change, and such a long passing of years? Seeing it submerged and harmless. She began to imagine that she was her brother, and that all the hugs pressed upon her semi-detached body were that impossible reconciliation.

'Who's that trip-trapping over my bridge!' Acantia cackled at Ursula, grinning in delight at her memories, knowing that Ursula shared them. Her eyes caught Ursula's in a swift, stabbing glance. *We have an understanding*, the eyes said, loving, accusing. *I can know all and forgive, see?*

The bridge led to a pergola that resembled other pergolas in some respects. In the old music room, or rather the ground over which it had stood, there was a large pond surrounded by rocks and plants filled with frightened fish. The walls had an austere beauty: expanses of marbled plaster streaked with black and pink sand patterns that were almost like watermarks. They had aged to a subtle grandeur.

Ursula stared up at the dead trunk of the apple tree. Its crabbed skeleton, broken at the crown, leaned and embraced the airy black spine and ribs of the dead deodar.

'I gave baked apples to all the guests at Siegfried and Isa's wedding!' Acantia giggled, putting a small hand over her broken teeth. Ursula laughed weakly. She could hear it as if she had been there. *Once in a lifetime apples! Baked on the tree! My house burned down just last week, you know!*

The fireplace was filled with dried flowers and ringed by candles. Where the kitchen had been, bright blooms of red and white were stark against the scarred and dappled walls. Ashes and roses, grey scars and geraniums. The walls were about shoulder height. Beate, looking in over them, resembled an impaled talking head. They all laughed. Parts of the ruins were staggered and each step had a pot of red geraniums bright against the black. The narrow chimney loomed tall into the crystalline sky. The old great hearth was quiet and silent but Acantia said they should come up in winter because there was no reason why they shouldn't light it as they had in the old days. They could have a winter barbecue.

Some parts had bits of roof built over them but most were open to the sky. Acantia had a picture-framing room, a room with shelves and the blackened Grimm and Andersen and other storybooks. Where the old study rooms had been, Pa had a beautifully restored music room painted in light cream and sandy tones which now housed the grand piano.

On the streaked and blackened walls of the kids' room, the giant cats that Acantia had picked out in the fire scars threaded themselves sinuously, emerging clearer when seen through the corner of the eye than when faced directly. Acantia also had a medicine room, lined with what looked like dried parsnips, some with two, three, even four hairy limbs. A weed had sprung up all over Whispers which Acantia named native ginseng and used in her potions and medications.

The Tarsinis were gone. They had severed themselves from their shadows. Where they had mimicked and ridiculed the Houdinis there was a great, square, empty space through which the tall children walked or jumped. No need for doors.

The auditorium, now the pergola, was Acantia's medicine wheel. Buoyed by their unconditional admiration for all she had done, she was leaping about eagerly to show everything. They stood on the Japanese bridge looking over the clay expanse of the pergola floor. It was in itself a painting rather like a mandala, made up of shells and rocks and sand, and with a self-seeded stringybark sapling rising from near the middle. Flowers ringed the outside, and stepping blocks of polished river redgum rounds led to the bridge. It was a dry marine world.

'Look!' she said, pointing. 'There in that galactic spiral is the story. The whole story of this house, if you know how to read it.'

'You have to be able to read Shell,' Helmut told Ursula, smiling.

Three spiral rays made out of a multitude of scallops and trails of pale sand radiated out from a small cairn in the centre, on top of which was a roughly pyramidal chunk of opal potch. Inside the cairn was a form of shrine containing a small wooden bowl and some other objects. Acantia leapt nimbly through the arms of the spiral.

'You go along here by this path and you can read the whole story inscribed in it. But if you cannot read, you do this.'

She reached into the cairn, into the bowl and brought out a small carved box which had survived the fire. She opened it and withdrew a crystal, which she thrust into Ursula's hands.

'Close your eyes!'

Ursula couldn't bring herself to. Acantia didn't notice.

'You can see the spiral, can't you? It is the wheel of the universe, centred on this home.' Her voice was reverent. 'From carbon comes diamond, and the miracle is the Connection!' She waved her arms above her head and twirled lightly on her toes, singing, '*Spiralling outward from the source of all Love.*'

Acantia told Ursula casually that she had discovered the secret of physical movement to the fourth dimension and that she and Pa had been there a couple of times. The medicine wheel and the story of the house were the great launching principles of all hyperspace travel and interdimensional transportation. She said that if Ursula cared to embark on a long course of purification she could come with them next time.

Acantia looked her in the eye mischievously this time, but still with a secret message.

Ursula noticed that Acantia had tears of happiness, or happy sadness, gleaming in her eyes as she smiled up at her children. Ursula had to walk away.

'It's feng shui,' Acantia was saying. 'Feng shui is used by most on *such* a small scale, but really we have to arrange the universe ourselves!'

Beate's house sagged next to the ruins in silent senility. It stank and everything in it was dirty or broken. Acantia and Pa had made it their own.

Siegfried was sitting on a log in the courtyard with Isa and their new baby. For most of them it was the first time they had met Isa, and they stared in grabs, glances and long draughts through half-closed eyes. Isa sat silent, prickly, warned, watchful, cradling the tiny creature in her arms. The baby had a hairline unheard of among the Houdinis. Siegfried had the aloof, easy air of someone who has a bodyguard. When Acantia settled down next to the mother and child, she had the look of a dog who almost dares to steal the dinner.

Acantia and Lilo sat talking in the courtyard that had been the kitchen. Acantia was laughing delightedly because they were almost talking about sex. She grabbed Lilo's hand and began reading her palm.

'Ooooh. You will marry five times, Lilo, five *different* men!'

Lilo snorted.

Helmut said, 'She's already had at least those five men.'

'Aaah, but these are special ones!'

'Obviously not special enough,' Lilo said.

Acantia giggled. 'Oh, men!'

Then she read Lilo's health.

'Mmmmm. *Sexually*, you are OK.'

'Yes. So I've been told.'

Helmut and Lilo exchanged glances, Lilo mischievous, Helmut laughing but uncomfortable.

Acantia shivered with delight.

In the corner of the kitchen that was, Helmut had built a small alcove by roofing the corner with gently sloping galvanised iron. It was beautifully done. It looked like a small stable or goat shed. It sheltered the great iron frame of the burned Lipp piano, strings intact, scarred picturesquely with charcoal; a nether-regions harp. As Pa lumbered about lighting candles for the Christmas carols, Acantia called the clan together theatrically by striking the harp and clashing two battered saucepan lids together.

They sang the old songs, the strange, sweet descant from Beate making the hair rise on the back of Ursula's neck.

Ehre sei Gott. Alles Schweiget.

Dona Nobis Pacem.

They sang into the descending dusk, sitting on logs where the table once was, sitting on the sill where the Tarsinis once lived. Acantia sat on a log, her legs tucked up to her chin, the white dress spattered with soup and streaked with charcoal. Ursula watched her mother's eyes touching the heads and bodies of her wild and vigorous children. Acantia's face was soft and gentle in the candlelight. Her cheeks flickered with orange and gold and blue and grey.

We have our snow on the inside had been a Christmas joke many years before. Ursula's heart was cold and empty, as ruined as the house. The golden chatter of her brothers and sisters rose around the shards of their past lives. She could hear them hidden around her, the children she had saved or perhaps stolen from her mother. She wanted to cry for Acantia, but could not.

As if in answer to her guilt and emptiness Helmut's voice rose in protest somewhere behind her.

'She loved us all. She did her best.'

Some glowing murmur soothed him and his voice fell down to earth once more.

Lilo, Siegfried and Ursula sat by the pond, laughing. The ruin was eerie and beautiful in the fading light. They listened to the others and themselves as several voices hummed and burbled, trailing upward from around the walls into the luminous dusk.

'It is a pity now that Gotthilf can't see this.'

'Certainly cleaned out the germs! Gotthilf can't use that argument any more to avoid bringing his kid here!'

'His imaginary kid.'

'Listen! It's silent!'

'It's a bloody Shrine of Forgetfulness!'

Arno came up and whispered, 'Where's the Aerogard hidden now?' He craned his neck over the parapet to make sure Acantia wasn't in earshot. None of them trusted whispers even now.

Ursula went out onto the restored verandah, the cats over her shoulders in the orange light behind her. The neighbours' trees in the foreground had grown so much that they obscured the nearby houses, but in the middle distance small farms, sheds and clusters of life were visible over the fields. The view was strikingly beautiful. Peaceful, harmonious. Toggenberg Hills hid the city with their soft and rounded peaks, patched with misted vineyards and cherry orchards. Mr Vatzek's growing herd of retired horses and crippled donkeys grazed down below the ruin in the field above the lake, their sleek bodies glowing orange and black. The fences were gone and dungheaps spotted the paddock almost up to the steps. She missed Gotthilf. She tried to imagine the man he might be. Golden-haired, dreamy, tap-tapping on his computer. The *novelist*. A hairy back, thirty-five years old. But she could only see the apparition of a skinny seventeen-year-old, glancing over his shoulder as he ran through the long grasses.

He had to love them all still. Did it show in that secret book? Books? Had he really written a book? If he had written the book she now knew in such detail, she knew that one day Gotthilf would have to tell them, maybe already had, in strange clues buried in his article and stories. She had copies in her bag. She had almost given everyone copies for Christmas, but hadn't found the moment. She was shy, hugely exposed by what the choice of her name really meant, even though none of them would guess.

Maybe tomorrow.

The verandah was scattered with masonite, paint and glue. Ranged along the wall were stacks of finished boards. Acantia had been painting as though possessed. She had said brightly after the fire that she would repaint all the old pictures. Scattered about the remains of the verandah were strange reflections of the old forms; ghost pictures, zombie pictures. Revenants with the once beautiful flesh hanging in murky shreds. All along the wall they marched, their forms sloppy, their perspective wonky, their colours dulled. Acantia had developed new techniques of mixing pigments using Liquid Nails. Cadmiums and Prussian blue were long gone.

Ursula became conscious after a while of a background noise. She could hear something scuttling, trickling along the walls. She turned, but there was nothing. Only the cats. But she could still hear it. It was a fragmented sibilant child's voice, one of their voices. It was singing with a lisp—

We are home
We are home

Home with the sailor home from the sea
Home is where you are meant to be
All that goes comes back to home

We are home
we are home
we are himmy home
we are home.

The sun was setting.

'Oh, did you know that the Count is dead? It's so sad!' Acantia didn't sound sad. She hadn't mentioned him for months. It was now an accepted fact that he was responsible for the fire. 'Yes, and he wasn't a count at all! . . . What? Oh no, we weren't *that* close to him.'

Her children were eyeing her stiffly, the atmosphere cold. Acantia flourished a newspaper clipping.

GRIMM MURDER: MACABRE FAIRYTALE KILLING

Named Nigel Hobbs on his birth and death certificates, Count Ugolini was found at the bottom of Sydney Harbour weighted down with rocks sewn into his emptied bowel cavity.

'I knew there was something fishy about him from the beginning!'

Ursula walked away with her skull empty. It was too much. Too recent, really, to begin to face any new facts to the story. Too soon to struggle against the new official version. *Gotthilf, Gotthilf! Please come back to this scarred graveyard!*

Beauty surrounded her but was held at a distance. She toyed with the word *disconsolate*, rolling it around the empty space, bouncing it against the walls, breaking it in two. This place was truly beautiful. This ruin seemed to record something that only Acantia ever saw.

'Don't worry,' Lilo said, clanking faintly as she wandered up from behind, 'we'll light a fire and have a toke later.' She went to get some oranges. Ursula tried to imagine bouncing oranges messily, juicily, smashing bright colours against the haggard walls.

What had it all been for? Where was a mark of the struggles and horrors these walls had seen? She stood in the centre of the house, its rooflessness giving her the feeling that it was shrunk in size, that it was a toy house in a sandpit and she had just stood up, brushed the sand from her knees and was about to step over its walls and away. It was even quaint. Where had the darkness and fear gone? Had it just been a long game or dream, something in their heads, a madness of time and place and isolation? It had burned just like any house would have, top off like an exploding kettle, guts open and leaping like popcorn. It had crisped to toffee like a marshmallow and left a sweet taste in Acantia's mouth.

A city was just twenty-five minutes away and her mother was a clinging tiny old woman who wore a mask of smiles over deep scars. The old, seeping horror crept over Ursula, and she slid towards the ancient question, waiting impassive as a guru in the darkness at the back of her mind.

Was it really Acantia who was mad and strange?

She felt each of her brothers and sisters sitting in their little compartments at the back of her skull. You could not tell that Beate was one-and-a-half-handed. She laughed in a high voice, loved her children crushingly. Gotthilf snarled from his recently opened tomb, guarding the entrance, hiding his child (did he really have a child?) and his book (a book?). Ursula was there, struggling to like sex and not to lose Speed, reading Vincent Buckley, Patrick White, Christina Stead, Xavier Herbert, dreaming not of a new family but of the old one. Siegfried, recalcitrant, by choice unemployed, was throwing his laughing baby into the air and catching her. Helmut, born again, was honouring his mother and father, bringing them pots of honey from his hives. Lilo was sitting cross legged polishing her knives, cleaning the barrel of her shotgun, surrounded by her beasts. Arno was wandering endlessly from cave to cave, straining to hear something he had not yet heard and reminding them all which day it was and which ones it resembled from the past.

They were all so normal. There was no evidence that anything, anything at all, had really happened.

It had certainly ruined her Christmas.

She went and sat on a log at the edge of the abandoned goats' paddock. It was overgrown with bracken and whisperweed, filled with rubbish that rivalled the rubbish they themselves had unearthed decades before. She tried to imagine Gotthilf sitting here back then, but found she couldn't. An ancient, intimate feeling crept over her, as if it had been waiting for her to sit still. *Filthy Ursula*. She felt it creep into her as if fingering her first slyly and then possessively between the legs. It was so long ago, and so profoundly familiar, this feeling. She wasn't surprised, somehow, that its half-life was so long, that it had waited like a hidden vapour, an infection, overlaying everything here. And she felt, for the first time in years, that she really was connected somehow with that child, that teenager she had once been. She let self-disgust wrap around her, feel her up, test her. It was almost voluntary—she was trying it on as one might to see whether a child-bride's wedding dress still fitted. She sensed that it was weakened, and that she only had to throw it off and walk away from this lilliput to be free of it again. She nearly laughed, even though her heart was thumping, and with a certain prescience she thought she ought to get up before she felt the full punch of that time. Then she suddenly passed out and fell back off the log into the bracken over the old goat's grave.

She came to quickly, disoriented, her heart racing. She was terrified for a moment that, supine, she was hopelessly vulnerable, and had a boiling feeling in her head that she had to run and run. She stayed there, staring up through the clots of pine needles at the sky and slowly calmed down. For the first time, then, she looked down at her body, her adult body, and thought:

It was me he took. He fucked me.

She could see it and feel it and remember it with absolute clarity, distinct and freed from the usual formulaic collection of words that she had used for years to signify it. For a blinding moment, it seemed real and huge, looming over, shadowing even her betrayal and loss of Gotthilf.

'Come to think of it,' she said out loud half an hour later, 'all in all—it was not all that good.'

Gotthilf would never come back here. She'd have to go find him, no matter what it took, clock him one over the head for using her name, and then . . . then they might be friends.

The next morning Acantia came and sat with the children on the logs in the kitchen that was. She looked tormented and square-eyed and the children tensed, bracing themselves. She sat too close to Beate, and then too close to Siegfried. Siegfried fell silent, got up abruptly and walked to the window space. Acantia grabbed Lilo by the waist, laughing gaily, and sat her youngest daughter down beside her, bodies touching.

'Let me look again!' she grabbed Lilo's hand, making exaggerated gestures and pulling faces. She looked up at everyone, laughing again, gripping tightly onto Lilo's hand. No one relaxed.

'Lilo is her mother's daughter! The very spitting image of me at her age! Let me see! Let me see!' She pulled Lilo violently, bringing the hand in her grip up close. 'How many children does she have, hey? How many *children*? Might it be *seven*?'

Everything seemed grey to Ursula. Acantia was wearing the

same dress as the night before, now settling rapidly into the class of the once-white.

Then Lilo said, 'Drop dead,' and got up and began to walk away.

Acantia stood up, shaking, her mouth making a little black love heart. Then she screamed in her voice from above: 'You stop right there, sick missy!'

Lilo barely faltered in her stride.

Acantia turned on the rest of her seated, stony-faced children. Her eyes were wild and spittle flew from between her broken teeth.

'You unnatural brood. Ah! Look at you sitting there eating drinking. Ah! Up here for Christmas never any other visits you come here to see each other what a cruel joke on Pa that you don't even care enough for him to come here and talk to him all he wants is for you to know him for who he is now! Ah! What sort of people *are you*?' She paused.

'You do not love me, no, not one of you. Mandrakes! You will suffer all your lives when I am gone!' Tears were running from her crushed face. Ursula almost thought to comfort her but was cut short.

'You!' She swung her fierce and burning gaze on Ursula. 'The suffering you have caused is unimaginable but always Pa and I have forgiven you! We forgive you! You destroyed this family! You! Rotten and evil. None of them will thank you for turning them from their *own mother*! Carrion crow! Leave! Who wants you? Get out Get out Get out! Oh! How is it that you are such hard and cold children? It wasn't from us! You didn't get it from us!'

Acantia rushed off through the trees gasping, and Ursula vomited into the grey, ruined fireplace.

Beate, Ursula, Siegfried, Isa, Arno and Helmut stared at each other in silence. Ursula wiped her arm against her mouth.

'Do you think there will still be a Christmas dinner?' Arno asked.

Siegfried shook his head. 'Nup.'

Lilo's F100 pick-up fired up loudly from the other side of the wall. A current rippled through them.

'I'm staying,' Helmut said, scandalised. Beate looked torn and bewildered but barely needed an explanation. It was hard to be the visitor from overseas.

Lilo crunched the gears trying to slam the pick-up into first. Siegfried, Ursula and Arno were stung into action, stampeding through the kitchen, past the medicine wheel, over the redgum planks and into the back of the pick-up. Isa kissed Beate briefly and followed with the baby. Beate held her maimed hand up in stiff salute.

They roared off, trailing a giant plume of yellow dust and grit. They didn't see Pa, standing alone among the twisted trees of the dying orchard. His hands hung like dead paws by his sides. He watched the flying hair and shining eyes of his children until the dust obscured them.

coda

'Oh, Ursa,' Acantia sighs. 'The way out of anything will always be up there.' She slaps Ursula's forehead with the palm of her hand, knocking Ursula backward a little off the branch, and then catching her. Ursula laughs. She knows what Acantia means.

'What do you mean?' she asks innocently.

'The Power of Art,' Acantia says dreamily and suddenly Ursula is unsure.

They are sitting together on a branch halfway up a giant radiata. Acantia puts her arm around Ursula's little, wiry body and Ursula stiffens with delight.

'What do you mean?' she asks softly, softly, controlling her breathing, making sure she doesn't sniff her snot up or spit.

'The Imagination, Ursula! No walls, no torture, can take that away.'

The tree sways slightly, like a stiff gentleman too proud to bow. They are level with the point where the smoke dissipates into the air, rising from the chimney way below. They sit on the branch, two fat birds who cannot fly. Then Ursula sees an angel, holy wings outspread, hovering above the smoke, garments glittering in the bright air. It is giving her the eye.

'Do you see that?' she gasps, sniffing and pointing. 'An angel! The angel!'

'Oh, Ursula. Imaginitis.' Acantia sighs heavily, scrapes Ursula's arms off her neck and climbs down, branch by branch, without looking up.

The angel is gone as if it had never been.